# THE WEDDING FLIGHT

## THE ALMOST WIVES CLUB, BOOK 4

## NANCY WARREN

AMBLESIDE PUBLISHING

ISBN: ebook 978-1-928145-20-2

ISBN: print 978-1-928145-18-9

Cover Design by Kim Killion

*Ambleside Publishing*

One Matchmaking
Wedding Gown, Five Brides.
Who will wear this enchanted gown down the aisle?
The Almost Wives Club

# CHAPTER 1

egan O'Reilly was strolling down Melrose Avenue on her lunch break when she fell in love. It wasn't just a passing fancy, or a sudden crush that would come and go in an instant; it was full-blown, smack you in the face and knock you out love with a capital *L*.

She walked those few blocks so often that she knew most of the window displays by heart. So she always took notice when a display changed. Joe's Past and Present was a vintage store that she'd been to a couple of times. Their content was well curated, offering everything from designer resale to the kind of quirky stuff that anybody shopping thrift stores or yard sales might stumble across if they had a good eye. But she'd never seen a window like this.

It wasn't a man she fell in love with. It was a dress. Not just any dress, but a romantic fantasy made real. The wedding gown seemed to be calling to her. From the pearls on the bodice to the graceful folds of the skirt, everything about it said, "Yes, Meg O'Reilly, I am yours." She had a momentary fantasy that stepping into that dress would be akin to waving a magic wand, or Dorothy snapping the heels of her sparkly red shoes together. A fantasy that could change reality in a moment. It wasn't that she was desperate to get married, but she was a single woman struggling in LA. It wasn't that easy to meet people, and she didn't make much money as a literary agent's assistant.

The gown shimmered with the promise of everything from Prince Charming to an easy life. All she had to do was walk in and try it on.

She stepped closer, so close that her nose butted the window. There was no price tag visible, which seemed like it might be bad news. That gown hadn't been thrown together by some girl who'd purchased a sewing pattern and a few yards of silk, and ran it up on her mother's old Singer. Everything about that dress screamed high-end couture.

The window display fascinated her. When she finally tore her eyes away from the wedding dress that held center stage, she noticed a series of bridesmaid gowns surrounding it like ladies in waiting before a queen. They ranged from flirty blue cocktail dresses to elegant sheaths, in every shade from reds through pinks and purples, all the way to black and white. She wondered if this was a sample sale because every gown seemed to be in the same size. Fascinated, and with not a lot else to do, she stepped inside the store.

A bell jingled as she walked in, and even the bell made her want to smile.

There were a couple of other customers browsing but it wasn't very crowded. She wandered through the store, pausing at various racks, her hands flipping through blue jeans that she didn't need, over to a huddle of tweed jackets. She walked deeper into the store to where an entire section was devoted to bridal wear. These gowns seemed as though someone's mother had been saving their dress for them and the bride had said, as tactfully as possible, "No thank you." None of them called to her.

There was a youngish guy behind the counter, his eyes

glued to a computer screen. He was cute. As though he felt her gaze on him, he looked up. "Can I help you?" He was tall, lean, and rangy. He wore a simple black T-shirt and jeans. His hair was brown and a little shaggy. He had one of those not-quite-beard things that could either be carefully manicured every day, or else he was too lazy to shave on a regular basis. Something about this guy suggested laziness rather than a need to be pretty. He had a high forehead and full lips, but it was the eyes that got her. They were gray-green, and when they focused on her she felt like she was the only woman in the world.

No, he couldn't help her. No one could help her. She was having some kind of psychotic breakdown. But, even as she realized her behavior was insane, she said, "Yes. Can you tell me about that wedding dress in the front window?"

His gaze sharpened on her. "You've got a very good eye. Have you heard of the designer, Evangeline?"

"Vaguely." She thought about it. She had heard the name recently; since she worked in publishing, she tried to keep up on blogs and gossipy websites—and then it came to her. "She's a wedding gown designer, but I think the business is in trouble."

"I don't think so. Do you know what an original goes for?"

"If you say it like that, I'm pretty sure I can't afford one."

She took a step backwards, ready to flee, and he stepped out from behind the counter. He was the sexiest vintage-store guy she'd ever come across. He said, "It doesn't cost anything to try it on."

"I don't want to put you to any trouble."

"It's no trouble. It's not like there are twelve others in the back. If you want to try it on, I have to take it out of the window. Just give me a minute."

She watched, fascinated, as he reached in and lifted the gown with great care. Maybe it was her imagination, but she felt as though the dress swirled towards him almost as though it were dancing with him. He looked at her and looked at the dress. "It's about your size."

She glanced down at herself, "I'm not exactly dressed to try on a wedding gown." She wore Doc Martens on her feet, cropped black trousers, a gray T-shirt and a black linen jacket.

But, he'd taken the dress out of the window for her, so the least she could do was try the thing on. He wafted the dress through the air to the back where there were two changing rooms, each with a heavy red velvet curtain that pulled across a black iron rail. "If you need any help getting into the dress, I could call my mom, she's upstairs."

"Your mom?"

"Yes. She's the Joe of Joe's Past and Present."

"In my head I was thinking of you as Joe."

He grinned at her. "No, I'm Dylan." He held out a hand and she shook it.

"I'm Meg. I think I can probably get myself into the dress."

"No worries. Shout if you need any help."

She stepped into the alcove, fortunately large enough for her and the dress, and began to chuck off her clothes. Her skin tingled with excitement. She undid the tiny covered buttons on the back of the dress and stepped into it. All she had on was a pair of blue-and-white polka-dot panties, and fortunately a lacy bra. The dress smelled wonderful, like a wedding gown should smell—like flowers and hope. The silk caressed her as she slipped her arms into the sleeves and pulled the bodice up over her chest. This had to be the finest silk and lace, and although she was no expert in couture, she had a sneaking feeling those pearls were real.

She reached behind her and managed to get about a half-dozen of the tiny buttons closed and then gave up. The dress was modest enough that a man could help her finish the buttons. Since he worked in a vintage store that catered mainly to women, she imagined he was fairly accustomed to helping out with zippers and buttons.

She couldn't get a proper view of herself inside the dressing room so she pulled back the curtain and stepped out. Dylan wasn't exactly hovering, but he hadn't gone back to bury himself in his computer either. When she stepped out, he walked towards her and she felt the moment of impact as an expression that he could not disguise crossed his face. It was like that moment when a man looks at a woman and she can feel his attraction.

He whistled low. "I am not blowing smoke, that dress was made for you."

He took her hand and led her towards a triple mirror so she could see herself reflected on all sides. And when she saw herself in the mirror, she knew he was right. This dress could not have fit her better had it been sewn right onto her body. It was beautiful, and it made her beautiful. Her breath caught in a full-on princess moment.

"Let me help you with the rest of those buttons," he said, stepping behind her. She felt as though she could hear, faintly playing, the strains of "Here Comes the Bride." His hands were lean and strong and each time he hooked one of the buttons, she felt a shiver cross her skin. He didn't do anything to make what he was doing less than businesslike, but she felt an incredible pull, and unless she was wildly mistaken, he was feeling it too. She glanced up and their gazes connected in the mirror. And she felt again that punch, almost of recognition, like the moment when Sleeping Beauty wakes up to find a complete stranger has just kissed her and brought her back to life. *Damn, don't think about kissing him.* But even as she had the thought she saw his gaze drop to her lips. Wow, this was seriously crazy.

"I'm not sure my Doc Martens are exactly the right footwear for this gown."

He stepped back and surveyed her. "I think it's a bride's right to wear anything she wants to. And frankly, when you're in that dress, there is no way to screw it up." He suddenly cleared his throat and said, "So, when's the big day?"

She was twirling this way and that and she felt that the dress wanted to waltz her down the aisle to where a mysterious Prince Charming waited for her. In her sudden vision, of course, the mysterious Prince Charming looked very much like Dylan, a man she'd met about eight minutes ago.

"The big day?"

"Your wedding. When are you getting married?"

"Oh . . ." She had no idea what to say. She hadn't had a date in months, never mind a boyfriend. She was as far from engaged as a girl standing in a wedding dress could possibly be. Of course, now that he'd gone to all the trouble of getting the dress for her, she didn't want to tell him she was twirling around in a wedding gown under false pretenses, so she said, "We haven't set a date yet."

Maybe the first step to finding the right guy to marry was to buy a wedding dress. No, she was crazy, but she wasn't that crazy. Still, she said, "There's no price tag on the dress. Is that bad?"

"That dress is priced at five grand."

Her eyes opened wide and her jaw dropped. "Five thousand dollars?"

"Go look on Evangeline's website. She only makes one dress at a time. And for what they cost, you could buy a car." Then he thought about it and said, "Well, if it was my car you could buy about twelve of them."

She couldn't help but smile at him. "I could never afford that."

"Unlike Evangeline, we do deals in the store. And, since I have some pull with the owner, I could probably get you a screaming deal."

"Anything more than three figures is probably more than I can afford." She was so disappointed. "It was a nice fantasy."

She started to head back for the changing room and he said, "Wait."

"Right, the buttons."

"No. We're planning to do some advertising around this dress and the wedding display. And, like I said, that dress was seriously made for you. Have you ever done any modeling?"

She shook her head so her curls bounced. "I have definitely not ever done any modeling." She was slim enough, but not super tall and would never have considered herself pretty enough.. "This dress should be modeled by a top runway model."

"Maybe at a couturier show. But not in *Joe's Past and Present*. Trust me on this."

"Wow. You seriously use shoppers as models?"

"What better way to hit our target market? Of course we do."

While they had been speaking he'd slipped back behind the counter and pulled out a camera from a drawer below the vintage cash register. "Do you mind?"

"I'm modeling now?"

He laughed and shook his head. "I'll snap a few photos of you now, to show my mom and my aunt—they're the ones who own the store. And I will get back to you."

She wasn't sure. Partly because she did not want to model this dress so that someone else could buy it. She'd like to hide the gown away in a closet somewhere or slip it among the old velvet smoking jackets that probably no one ever touched, until such time as she actually had a groom and a wedding date and the funds to buy this wonderful gown. He must have seen the look of hesitation on her face because he added, "we don't pay you in money but you do get a pretty hefty store credit."

She perked up a little at that. "Really?" On her salary she even had to be careful shopping in vintage stores. "Okay."

She stood there while he snapped photos from several angles. He didn't ask her to smile or pose and she got the feeling he was more interested in how the dress looked on a human mannequin. Then he said, "Great, I'll undo those buttons now. And when you're finished come on out and you can leave your contact information with me."

She turned her back and he walked up behind her and once again she felt the impact as his fingers brushed her skin. The first button was at the top of her neck. When he touched her there she shivered. He'd been fairly swift and efficient doing up the buttons but his movements were a little more languorous now. It was as though he were undressing his bride. She had another one of those crazy visions, and instead of him standing at the end of an aisle, they were in a hazily outlined bridal suite. She could see the glow of candlelight highlighting a huge bed covered with lacy pillows. As he undid each button she grew increasingly lightheaded. Without even asking her, he undid them all the way to her waist. She held the bodice against her chest and said, "Thank you." And then she dove into the changing alcove and dragged the red curtain shut behind her. What had just happened? How could she feel turned on by a man she didn't even know who had undone a few buttons?

She needed therapy. Or an actual date. Carefully, she eased herself out of the gown and hung it on the padded hanger. She dragged in a deep breath after she had her street clothes back on, and said to her reflection, "Don't be an idiot."

Strong words, but they didn't have much impact. She stepped outside to see Dylan was back behind the counter. A customer was buying a heap of clothes and he was ringing them up. She walked up and with barely a glance he pushed a piece of paper and a pen to the edge of the counter. "If you could leave your contact information, I'll get back to you in the next couple of days."

He could be referring to a clothing item she was looking for and she appreciated that he wasn't making a big deal of her possibly modeling for the store. She nodded and wrote down her address. And cell number. Also, her email address. She contemplated adding her work number but that might be overkill. She didn't want to seem too eager.

She pushed the paper and pen back towards him and said, "Thanks. Talk to you soon."

And then she walked back onto Melrose Avenue, surprised to find the world was running exactly the way it always had.

DYLAN WEST PACKED up his current customer's purchases, then collected the wedding gown from the fitting room. He was putting it back in the display window when his mother walked up to him. "Did somebody try on the Evangeline gown? We only redid the display last night."

He was still trying to process what had happened. When had he become a man who fell instantly for a pretty face? On a woman who was engaged to another man? "Not only did she try the gown on, but seriously, it looked like the dress was designed for her."

"Then why didn't she buy it?"

"I don't think she can afford it."

"Too bad."

"I know. But, I was thinking. How often are we going to get a gown like this in stock? We should use this opportunity to do some advertising."

She glanced at him in surprise. "You've always said advertising is a waste of money. That we have our loyal clientele, our website and newsletter, and enough walk-in traffic that we don't need it."

He had a business degree from Stanford, a promising Internet start-up company in the planning stages, and he also had common sense. But he wanted to see Megan O'Reilly again. That was her full name. He'd checked out her information and immediately liked the loopy scroll of her handwriting. It was like she could form each letter as perfectly as an expert calligrapher, but she didn't have time. Her handwriting was quirky, like she was.

"I was thinking that, since this girl looks incredible in the dress, we might do a little feature around the Evangeline original and include a few of those bridesmaid dresses. We're in the middle of bridal season. Might help us move some of the wedding stock."

Joe always listened to him, but she also had strong opinions of her own. She'd been a successful model back in the seventies and eighties. She did a lot of complaining about contemporary models, especially the heroin-chic type. She asked, "Is she a professional model?"

"No. She's never modeled before." He went back and picked up the camera. "Take a look. I snapped some photos of her."

"Wow. You're really serious about this."

"I just got a feeling. Well, you'll see."

His mom took the camera but she looked at him first. Then she flipped through the four shots he had taken. "You're right," she said after she had studied them for a few minutes. "The gown was made for this girl."

"What do you think? Is she the right person to model it?"

"I think she's the right person to wear it down the aisle. Did you offer her a discount?"

"I did. I also told her that if she modeled for us we'd pay her in store credits."

His mom nodded. "Did she seem interested?"

"Yes, I think so. She left me her contact information."

"Well, if she models the dress for us and then puts her store credit towards buying it, we all win. You're right, this is great advertising for the store, and the dress is perfect for that girl. Maybe it's better that she's not a professional."

"Great." Of course, his mother was the one with all the connections in the fashion world, and she still kept up with her former agents as well as young models who often came to her for advice. She knew all the best photographers, the best stylists and makeup artists. In fact, she still turned down modeling jobs.

"Do you see this as online advertising or print?" Joe asked.

"I think we should put it on the website, and do some targeted online advertising. Maybe hit a few local blogs."

Joe nodded. "Okay. Let's do it."

He took the paper with Meg's details and handed it to his mom. "Megan O'Reilly. She looks like a Meg O'Reilly, doesn't she? There's definitely Irish blood in that girl."

She tapped her fingers on the page. "I'll get the photographer. What do you think about Saturday after we close? You should call her since she knows you."

She'd probably be out with her fiancé on a Saturday night, and Dylan had to keep reminding himself that she was an engaged woman. He tried to be cool about the thought of talking to her again. "I'll call and ask."

# CHAPTER 2

*W*hen Meg arrived home that night, she heard her roommate June talking. Meg stood and cocked her head, listening. If June had one of her friends over, she'd have to make small talk before escaping to her room. But, no. Within a minute she knew that June was running lines. Her roommate could never decide whether she wanted to be an actress or a writer. Of course, lots of people did both, but she was all one or all the other and could flit from one dream to the other with startling rapidity and no notice to her poor roommate. Meg recognized the play. It was *A Streetcar Named Desire*.

She walked into their living-room-slash-kitchen and found June wearing a slip and stomping up and down. "I'm Stanley Kowalski's wife," she said as Megan walked in.

"Stella!" Meg bellowed.

She tossed the script to the counter. "Probably some blonde with Polish blood will get the part."

June was half Chinese and half American, and complained about how hard it was to get parts as she was neither one nor the other. She wore her black hair long and worked out a lot. She also ran a blog, *Single Chick in LA*, where she dished about her dating life and poked fun at the men of LA. Of course, in order to get fresh material, she did a lot of dating. Sometimes, she tried to get Meg to go out too, as a research assistant.

June butted out her cigarette. Since she didn't smoke, Meg figured it was part of her getting into character.

"Where's the play?"

"In an experimental theater. So maybe they'll take a chance on a racially diverse Stella."

"What's experimental about doing Tennessee Williams?"

"It's a mash-up. Tennessee Williams and Shakespeare."

"Wow."

"Blanche and Ophelia, get it?"

She nodded. "Battle of the waifs." She put on the kettle to make tea. Her evening already felt heavy with manuscripts that she had to get through. In her agency, assistants got promoted to agents when they either landed a promising new client, or found a project that could be made into a movie. The big bosses were going to promote one of the assistants soon and Meg felt she was ready in every way, except that she hadn't yet found a big client or an impressive project. With each manuscript she read, she began with the hope that this was the one.

"When are you going to look at my novel?" June asked, seeing Meg's heavy bag.

This was not the first time they'd had this conversation. "Have you finished your novel?"

"If I had a contract I would finish it."

"And, if you finished it, it would be much easier to sell. Nobody buys a first novel unless it's finished."

June tossed her hair. "All anyone has to do is read my blog and they can see what my novel will be like."

"Please. Finish the novel."

"You are so anal." Then she said, "Hey, I have a surprise for you."

"You do?"

"Yes." She opened her laptop and motioned Meg over to the small couch. "I made this for you. Because, as a friend, I have to tell you, you need to get out more!"

It was an online dating profile. "Tell me that is not live," Meg cried in horror. "I've told you a million times I'm not interested in online dating."

"Come on. You've never even tried it. There's loads of great guys out there. You can't spend every night shut away in your room reading manuscripts that your boss doesn't want to represent."

"But that's the only way I'll get a promotion. I'll never get to be an agent until I convince the senior agents that I have an eye for talent."

"You're making excuses. You're young. You should get out and start dating."

She glanced at the site. "Cupid's Arrow? Seriously?"

"It's the best one in LA." She hit a couple of keys and a list of men's mug shots showed up. "Look. This guy would be perfect for you."

She stared at the picture of a really geeky-looking guy with heavy glasses and possibly the worst haircut in the greater LA area. "He says his hobbies are World of Warcraft and snooker. What on earth makes you think we would have anything in common?"

"Look at his job. He says he's in publishing and media. Like you are."

"That's what you put on your profile because you run your own blog. I am guessing that's what geek boy here does too."

"Look, if you're going to be picky you'll spend your whole life alone."

An image flashed across her mind of Dylan, the amazing guy she'd met in the vintage store. For a second she was tempted to tell June about him, and the weird breakdown that had led her to try on a wedding dress. But, knowing June, she'd use the experience in a blog post. So, instead she said, "I am starting to get out more. I joined a film club and a meet-up group for writers."

June made a rude noise. "Why would you go to a writers' group when you don't write? You're looking for the next *Divergent* or *Gone Girl*, you're not fooling me."

Damn. June had seen right through her. "You write. You should join the writers' group."

"I should."

Since June was passionately interested in both her careers, it was easy to get her sidetracked. "In fact, we should go together."

"Maybe." Then she turned back to the screen. "Anyway, here's your profile."

Meg stared at a picture of herself on the screen. "Where did you get that picture?"

"It's one I snapped when we were at the beach last weekend."

"You were taking a profile picture? You should have told me."

June shook her head. "Then you'd have gone all self-conscious and posey. I like this one. It's very natural and it shows you having fun. Which you never do."

"First, I do have fun, and second, I am not going on a dating site."

"I'm trying to help you."

"You're trying to get an extra correspondent for your blog. I am not going to date guys so you can make fun of them."

"That's harsh. I don't make fun of them."

She grabbed her own laptop, and pulled up June's blog. Oh, this was too easy. "'How to tell if you're dating a douche.' That is the title of your latest entry."

"Well, it's a public service. A woman should be able to tell if a guy's a douche before they get serious."

She continued, "Douchebaggery clue number one. He asks you if you like reading, and when you say yes, he shoves his latest screenplay, unfinished novel, or avant-garde poem in your face."

June at least had the grace to know when she'd been busted. She tried to keep her expression serious but the grin showed through. "Honestly, that actually happened to a friend of mine."

"That friend was me. This guy found out I was an agent's assistant. That's why he wanted to go out with me."

"Ouch. I forgot that was you."

"Really, I'm not doing this."

"Well, don't blame me when you're a lonely old spinster who's gone blind from reading too many unpublished manuscripts and whose only company is a mangy old cat."

"Warning taken."

Meg took her tea and her heavy bag containing a few printed-out manuscripts, her laptop, and her e-reader into her bedroom and shut the door. She spent a lot of time in here when she was home. It wasn't that she didn't like her roommate, because she did, but June always seemed to be trying to get her to do something. Either to go on a double date, to run lines, or to take her on as an agency client. It was easier sometimes to simply shut herself away. In her room, she could work uninterrupted.

A lot of agency submissions came electronically these days, so, often, instead of curling up with a book, she found herself curling up with her reading device. She had three manuscripts she wanted to take a serious look at tonight. She opened the first. Within two pages she knew there wasn't much hope. The writer could not spell, had no idea about character development and was pretty much putting her own spin on *The Hunger Games*. She read fifty pages because that was her cutoff point. If she'd read that far, she could feel justified in turning something down.

Of course, in her wildest dreams, she wouldn't even know what page she was on. She'd be so engrossed in the story she could not stop reading. But, the truth was, those reads were few and far between.

She was on page forty-eight and really thinking that for once she might break a rule when June called from the other room: "Your phone is ringing!"

She glanced up. She hadn't even noticed that she'd left her purse, containing her phone, in the kitchen.

"Coming."

She got off the bed and padded to the main room. June was holding her phone. "It was Dylan. Who do you know named Dylan?"

In the same moment she felt a giggly excitement that Dylan had already phoned her. And irritation that June was holding her phone. She said, "My phone was in my purse."

"I know. I heard it ringing so I took it out for you."

"Why?"

"Because if it was your boss I would answer it."

She really needed to make sure and bring her personal items into the bedroom with her at all times. "No. You will not answer my phone if my boss calls. If he calls looking for me and you start pitching your unfinished book, all you'll do is piss him off and then he'll never look at your manuscript."

June shrugged. "I probably wouldn't have anyway. So? Who's Dylan?"

"A writer we might sign," she lied. "With a finished manuscript."

"Is he cute?"

The vision of all that shaggy gorgeousness flashed before her. She kept her gaze on her phone. "He's okay."

"Damn. If you ever get a really hot one, call me."

June had changed into high-heeled black boots, which she wore with a short black dress. She'd put her hair up. "Date night?"

"Yep. He's an actor, too. You never know."

"Plus, it's all good material for your blog. Or your novel."

"I am looking for the real thing, you know. Deep down. But, until Mr. Right shows up, blogging about the crazy things that happen to me keeps me sane."

"I know. Have fun."

She waited until she heard the front door click, then ran to the window to make absolutely sure that June had not forgotten anything and wouldn't be returning to the apartment. Then she picked up her phone. She listened to the message but all it said was, "Hi, Meg. This is Dylan from Joe's Past and Present. We were talking about you modeling for us. Can you give me a call back?"

Should she call right away? Or should she act cool and wait for tomorrow. Then she shook her head at her own foolishness. What was she doing? This wasn't a date. This wasn't a guy she was interested in—well, yes she was, but he didn't know that.

Anyway, she'd never been able to figure out the ins and outs of when you were supposed to call, so she returned the call right away.

He picked up with flattering speed: "Hi." She liked his voice. It was deep and a little bit rough.

Her lips curved. "Hi," she said.

"So, I talked to Joe and she checked out your photos. She agrees that you would be a great model for the dress. Are you still interested?"

In truth, she was more excited about seeing Dylan again, but the thought of sliding into that magical dress did appeal. She said, "Yes. I am."

"Fantastic. I forgot to ask you when you're available?"

"I work regular hours. Monday to Friday nine to five." In truth, it was a lot closer to eight to six.

"Great. Would you be available this Saturday? We close at five on Saturdays so if you came at six, that would give us time to set up."

Wow, they moved fast in the vintage store business. "I'll check my calendar."

She looked at her calendar and it was as blank on Saturday night as she had remembered that it would be. She said, "Yes. That looks fine."

"Fantastic. Why don't we say six at the store and if I need to change the time I'll let you know."

"Fine." He knew she had never modeled before but she felt she should ask, "Do I need to do anything or bring anything?"

"No. Just come as you are. We'll bring in a hairstylist and makeup artist."

"Wow. This is the big time."

"Not really. We'll put the photos on our website and do some advertising online. Nothing too fancy."

She was relieved to hear it. Low key meant there was less to be nervous about. "That sounds fine."

"I'll see you on Saturday."

She felt as excited as though the hottest guy in the world had singled her out and asked her for a date. Even though, of course, that wasn't true. For all she knew, Dylan was married with six kids. No. He couldn't be. She had certainly taken note that he wore no wedding ring. And, something about him screamed single. She wanted to think it was the way his fingers had brushed her skin and the way her body had responded.

# CHAPTER 3

*S*aturday morning, Meg took herself to a yoga class, hoping it would calm the butterflies—make that elephants—in her stomach. She didn't know whether she was more nervous about modeling and having her photograph taken or the thought of seeing Dylan again. Instead of feeling meditative and at one with her body, she spent most of the yoga class hoping she wouldn't screw up her modeling assignment.

After class, she was walking home and passed a nail salon. On impulse she went in and had her nails done. When she got home, she had a couple of manuscripts to go through and then she began getting ready for Joe's.

June came flying in just as she was getting ready to leave. She wore her best jeans and a shirt in her favorite blue. She had washed her hair but left it hanging loose since a stylist was coming. Even though Dylan had told her a makeup artist had also been hired, she put a little light makeup on anyway because she didn't want Dylan to see her at her plainest. June said, "Hey, you look nice. Where you going?"

Damn. She had hoped she and June would miss each other

today. She always tried not to lie, so she said, "Oh, just a work thing."

She could justify that this was a work thing since she was going to do a task for which she would be paid. Sort of.

June looked at her sharply. "Is this like a cocktail party with agents and people who might like to buy my book?"

"No. It's not. And where is this book you want people to buy?"

"I'm working on it. I'm an artist. You can't rush these things."

"Well, when your muse spends long enough in your presence that you can actually write this book, then you will give it to me, and I will go through it. We are not sending it to my boss or anyone else until it's ready to go."

June fiddled with her earring. "I think I have writer's block."

She really had no time for this, but June was a good friend in her own way. "And what are the symptoms of this writer's block?"

"I keep getting stuck."

Even though she wasn't the most experienced literary agent, she knew all about writers and their insecurities. She said, "Here's what I think. If you sit and start writing, you'll get unstuck. Try interviewing one of your characters or do a writing exercise in one of those how-to books on your shelf."

June was always so confident, but suddenly she looked uncertain. "What if it's no good? I've been talking about writing for so long, it's my dream. Well, one of my dreams. What if I can't do it?"

"That's good old fear of failure. Not writer's block. You have to write the book that's in you. And then you edit it to make it better. Being a novelist isn't all cocktail parties and book launches, you know. It's hard work."

"I guess."

"So, where are you off to?"

June forgot her artistic torment and perked up. "I have the hottest date tonight. His pictures look so drool-worthy that he's bound to be a serial killer." She got to her bedroom and turned, "Or married."

"So long as he's not both."

"Have fun tonight."

"You too."

She arrived at Joe's a couple of minutes early. Since she didn't want to appear too eager, she applied fresh lip-gloss and ran a brush through her hair one more time. Then, she took a deep breath, and pushed through the doors. The bell jingled, and she headed deeper inside. She was impressed at what they had done in an hour. The bridal wear had been cleared from the back alcove and in the space, an antique red velvet settee with gold-scrolled arms and back was settled in front of a huge white screen. Big lighting umbrellas and large and very professional-looking cameras were already set up.

The sofa sat on top of some kind of white fabric, so it had a dreamy, airy look to it. Dylan caught sight of her and came forward. A grin spread across his face and she thought he was happy to see her. The way her heart banged against her ribs, she knew that she was very happy see him, too.

"Hey," he said. "You made it."

"I did."

"Come and meet my mom. She's upstairs."

He led her behind the cash desk to a door that he opened, revealing a flight of stairs. He ascended and she followed. He called out, "Mom, Meg is here."

When she reached the top of the stairs she found herself in a cozy apartment. It was simply furnished and contained a few mannequins and racks of clothing. The woman who walked forward to greet her had an arresting face, with amazing cheekbones and huge eyes. She had to be six feet tall, and was dressed all in black. She looked Meg up and down, then said, "It's nice to meet you."

"You too."

She turned to speak to someone behind her, a short blonde woman wearing tight jeans and a T-shirt advertising a band Meg had never heard of. She said, "Nikki, check out this hair and these eyes."

Meg had always been slightly embarrassed about her eyes. They were dark brown but close together so that when she looked in the mirror she always thought she looked slightly cross-eyed. But the two women didn't seem to think so. "Oh, what I can do with those eyes. They're fascinating. The color and the depth—I'm thinking smoky shadow, maybe some gold." She patted Meg. "We're going to have some fun."

Yet another person came forward. Joe introduced her as Gabriella, the hairstylist. She was from Argentina and around Meg's age. Gabriella pushed her hands into Meg's hair, arranging it one way and then another.

Dylan watched for a moment and then said, "I'll be downstairs if anyone needs me."

For the next forty-five minutes, Meg was creamed and powdered and made up. She'd never had a professional makeup application before, so it was strange to feel like a canvas being painted with no idea of the results. The hairstylist meanwhile seemed quite accustomed to working at the same time as a makeup artist and she found herself wearing hot rollers while her eye makeup went on, and then having her hair combed out before Nikki put the finishing touches on her lips and cheeks. Gabriella said to Joe, "Do you want the hair up?"

Joe narrowed her eyes and considered. "I don't want anything too formal. Can you do a sort of updo with curls spilling down?"

The woman nodded briskly. "What I'm thinking myself."

When the hair and makeup were done, Joe asked "What size are your feet?"

"Size seven."

"I've got some pretty silver shoes that are an eight. Maybe a nine. They'll do. It's not like you have to walk."

Finally, she was allowed to rise from her sitting position and Joe helped her into the wedding gown. This time, she'd at least had the sense to slip into some pretty underwear. The woman efficiently did up all the covered buttons at the back and she couldn't help but recall how much nicer it had been when Dylan did them for her.

Joe stepped back and looked at her from top to bottom. Then she smiled. "Yes," she said. "Yes."

It was Gabriella, the hairstylist, who led Meg to a full-length mirror and said, "What do you think?"

What she thought, for one surreal moment, was that someone truly had waved a magic wand. Her hair was like something out of a magazine. It rose on top of her head in a coppery twist while a couple of curls touched her cheeks and one lay against her shoulder. Her hair was both sexy and romantic at the same time, and what Nikki had done with her makeup was amazing. Where she always played down her eyes, Nikki had emphasized them with eyeliner, smoky shadow, and a touch of gold.

Her cheeks were faintly flushed and her lips looked full and silky under a pale pink lipstick. Finally, she felt that she looked pretty enough to wear this gown. In fact, she had never felt so pretty in all her life.

That magical wedding gown urged her to throw caution to the winds, to dance through life instead of putting one foot ahead of another, cautiously, as she always had done.

"The shoes are downstairs, and the photographer should be all set up by now," Joe said. "Let's go."

She floated down the stairs in her stocking feet. And when

she got back into the main store, Dylan turned to look at her. She felt the impact as he took her in. His jaw didn't drop, exactly, but she knew she'd blown him away. He stepped forward hastily. "You look beautiful," he said.

His mother overheard him and she said, in a slightly acidic tone, "Yes, Meg. When you get married you'll have to make sure to get your hair and makeup done in a similar fashion. I'll give you both Nikki and Gabriella's cards if you're interested."

Dylan blinked and took a step back at his mother's words.

She wanted to cry out, "No, it's not true. I'm not engaged." But she couldn't. There was a reason she never told lies: she was no good at it. Now she had to let Dylan think she was engaged or risk looking like a fool.

Joe's cell phone rang and she said, "Good, the rest of the girls are here." She walked to the front of the store and let them in and brought them back to where the photographer was posing Meg in front of the screen.

Four tall, thin young women who all walked like dancers arrived and seemed to know everyone. Except Meg.

They'd arrived already looking camera-ready with hair and makeup done. Joe sent them upstairs anyway where Nikki and Gabriella would touch them up. The selection of bridesmaid dresses was also upstairs and the real models, as Meg thought of them, would wear those.

Joe had told her that she'd invited four aspiring models to take part in the shoot. It was a great way for them to get portfolio pieces and some practice. They'd also get store credits instead of cash.

The photographer had Meg stand here and there, and put her arm in this position or that, and an assistant would run around and make sure the dress draped properly. It would have been pretty boring except that she could see Dylan behind the scenes watching. "Imagine you're a woman in love," the photographer directed.

With Dylan in the background it wasn't so hard.

When Joe returned with the four bridesmaids, they all posed together until Joe stopped the shoot.

"Too much estrogen."

Everyone stared at her.

"A bride needs a groom," she stated and then turned to Dylan, "Where's the Armani tux that we got in a couple of weeks ago?"

"In the rack of men's formalwear," he said in a flat tone. "Why?"

"Because I want you to put it on and pose with the girls."

"I've always said he should model," said one of the bridesmaids. Meg thought her name was Laci, but they'd been introduced so fast she wasn't sure. Laci, or whatever her name was, looked like she'd be happy to do a lot more than pose with Dylan. Meg knew exactly how she felt.

"And I've always said no," Dylan replied firmly.

"Dylan, this was your idea," his mother reminded him, "and every bride should have a groom."

She thought he was going to refuse and then he looked over and their gazes connected. She thought that Dylan standing beside her in a tux, while she modeled this fabulous gown, would complete her fantasy. Maybe instead of payment she should ask for one of the photographs. She thought she'd keep it forever, and, if June was right, which she probably was, and Meg ended up a sad old spinster, at least she could show the cats her one shining moment.

He mumbled something, and then headed off into the store and in a few moments returned holding a gorgeous black tuxedo. "You know it's too big."

"Do you think I modeled for fifteen years without knowing how to make clothes look like they fit?" his mother asked. She walked upstairs and he followed, carrying the tux. While they were gone, the photographer snapped a few more shots of her and her bridesmaids and then Dylan strode in wearing the designer tuxedo. He looked amazing. Tough and rugged in that perfectly tailored suit. His eyes glowed green like a gorgeous jungle cat's.

Dylan settled beside her on the couch. "Good," Joe said. "You make a very handsome couple."

He grinned at her, showing even white teeth, and she couldn't help but smile back. She heard the click of the camera shutter.

"We need some action, some romance," the photographer said.

For a moment Dylan's gaze slipped to her lips and she thought, oh, yeah, some action would be good. Then Joe's voice intruded. "Good idea. What about a ring. Why don't you put a ring on her finger?"

She had never been so glad that she had taken the time to have a French manicure. Especially when Joe inspected her hands and she had the pleasure of knowing she had made one former model very happy. "Oh, perfect. Let me look in the vintage jewelry case and I'll see what I can find."

She returned a couple of moments later with two sets of rings. "I notice you don't wear an engagement ring?"

"No," she said. And then she racked her brain for a reason why an engaged woman would not be wearing a ring. "We haven't picked one out yet." That sounded reasonable.

"In the meantime, do you mind wearing this one?"

It was a vintage engagement ring, and she loved it immediately. It was a simple platinum band with a line of diamonds in a Deco style. She imagined this ring was exactly what she'd have chosen if she were engaged. "It's so beautiful," she gasped.

"We have a small selection of jewelry. I only take in pieces I love," Joe admitted. "It has a matching band. The rings probably won't fit you, but that doesn't matter."

She handed Dylan the engagement ring and he practiced

slipping it onto the ring finger of her left hand. The ring, like the dress, fit perfectly. This was getting spooky. The ring winked up at her from her newly manicured hands.

"Now, Dylan," the photographer said as Joe handed him the wedding ring and stepped away. "I want you to slide that ring onto her finger and look at her as though she is the woman you've been waiting for your whole life."

"That won't be difficult," he said, but so softly she wasn't sure she'd heard him correctly. When he raised her hand, she felt she was trembling. His hand was so warm and steady. He took the ring and slowly slipped it onto her finger, all the while looking deeply into her eyes.

She knew they were changing the level of the lights, and she heard the click of the camera, but all she saw was him.

"Oh, my," Nikki said, standing beside Joe to watch. "That is so romantic I think I'm going to cry."

The photographer said, "Dylan, this time I want you to lift your bride up. Scoop her up in your arms, let's see if we can get the action in the movement. I want the maids gathered round and watching."

"Ready?" Dylan asked her.

"As I'll ever be."

The photographer got set up and then said, "Whenever you're ready."

Dylan scooped her up in his arms. Oh, she wanted to stay there forever. Without even being directed to, she leaned her cheek against his shoulder and one arm crept round his neck. She felt him breathing, his chest rising and falling, she felt that he would never drop her once he had her in his arms. She was as weightless a soap bubble.

The camera snapped. The moment stretched. And then, suddenly, it was over.

The photographer said, "I think we got some great shots. Joe, anything else you'd like to see?"

"No. If you're happy, I'm happy."

Meg wanted to throw out some ideas simply to keep the shoot going, but of course she didn't. And, like every perfect dream, this one ended. Joe led her back upstairs, and once more helped her with the tiny buttons. She got back into her street clothes. The last thing she did was slip those beautiful rings off and give them back.

"You did a great job. You're really natural with the camera. Would it be okay if we call you again?"

"Oh, yes. I really had a good time."

She went downstairs and she thanked both the makeup artist and hairstylist. "You made me look so pretty," she said, still amazed at the transformation.

Nikki said, "All we did was make you look more like yourself." Then she added, "Here's my card. I'd be happy to do your makeup for your wedding."

She felt like a horrible person letting these nice women believe she was getting married. "Thank you." If she ever did get married she'd definitely call Nikki and Gabriella.

She was almost ready to go, but she couldn't leave without saying goodbye to Dylan. Of course, he had to change as well. She chatted pointlessly with the photographer for a couple of moments and then, when she couldn't think of another inane question to ask, she heard pounding feet on the stairs and the next thing Dylan was back in his jeans and shirt looking like himself again.

"Oh, good," he said. "You're still here."

She felt herself blush. "I was just leaving."

"Right. Saturday night. You probably have plans." Was it her imagination or did he look disappointed?

"No," she said eagerly. "No, actually I don't."

"Aren't you seeing your boyfriend? I mean your fiancé?"

"No. He's, um, out of town."

"Well, I don't know about you, but I never had dinner. Do you want to grab something?"

Oh yes, oh yes, she wanted that about as much as she wanted the earth to keep turning. She said, "That would be great."

He said a casual goodbye to everybody and then held the door open as she walked out ahead of him.

# CHAPTER 4

"There's an Argentinian place just down the block. Will that be all right?" he asked her.

"Yes, that sounds perfect."

She felt good just walking beside him. They chatted about the photo shoot and dodged pedestrians. And then they were there.

The restaurant was busy on a Saturday night but they were able to get a table for two in the center.

He said, "I can recommend the steaks, the sangria, and the empanadas. That's all I've ever eaten here, but probably everything is good."

A skinny guy who looked more Cuban than Argentinian came by their table. "What can I get you folks?"

She was too nervous to choose food. She said, "Empanadas and sangria sounds amazing."

Dylan nodded, "Make that two."

"Glass of sangria or a jug?"

"We're celebrating," he said. "Make it a jug."

When the sangria arrived it glowed deeply red and was full of fruit. Their waiter poured them their first glass and Dylan raised his and said, "To the prettiest bride in Los Angeles." The waiter was still in earshot. He turned, and said, "You guys engaged? Congratulations."

She blushed and shook her head. Dylan was a lot cooler. He said, "She's engaged to another guy."

The waiter looked at the two of them and shook his head. "Bad luck, man."

Dylan chuckled. "Tell me about it."

For a woman who hadn't dated in almost two months, this was too much.

She glanced up and caught his gaze on her and quickly turned her attention back to her drink. There was a tiny pause and then he said, "So, tell me about yourself."

She hated that question because the answer was so uninteresting. "I think I've lived the most boring life in history," she said at last. "I grew up in Northern California. I have one brother. My dad is a pilot and my mom is a schoolteacher." She paused. "I won a spelling bee in fifth grade."

He chuckled. "And you say you haven't led an exciting life?"

She began to relax. He was so easy to talk to and he seemed genuinely interested in her boring life. She continued, "I always loved to read and so I studied English literature in college. I planned to be a teacher like my mom but I'm more interested in books than kids. I decided to move to LA or New York and get a job as an editor. But an opportunity came up here in LA for an agent's assistant at a really good literary agency, and I thought, why not? I got the job and I've been there almost two years."

"That's cool. Do you represent anyone famous?"

She shook her head. "Well, our agency does. But my job is mostly to read through all the submissions. I'm looking for two things: first, authors that we might like to represent, and second, books that might make good film or TV."

"I'm guessing it's a good thing you love reading."

"Honestly, we're so busy in the day dealing with the clients we have that I do most of my reading on my own time. But I keep hoping and dreaming that one of those books will be the one. You know, the book that makes the difference. That could become a classic."

His eyes twinkled, but she saw sympathy there. "And how's that going for you?"

"It's like everything else. There's a reason a book becomes a classic. It says something new, or says something profound in a way that's never been said before, and you read it and you say, yes, that's how life is." She shrugged. "There are not a lot of books like that coming in the slush pile at my agency."

"Is that important to you? To find the next great novel?"

"That's how I'll get promoted. They're going to create a position for another agent, and there are three of us who all want it. The one with the best clients or who signs a successful project is probably going to get the job."

"Sounds like stiff competition."

"It is."

"What is your favorite book?"

She didn't hesitate. "*Pride and Prejudice.*"

A look of pain crossed his face. "Is that the one where the hot Brit guy jumps in the pond so his shirt becomes see-through?"

She shook her head vehemently. "That's a modern TV adaptation. I'm talking about the original Austen novel. Brilliant social satire with a fantastic love story."

"What is it with women and romance?"

"Let me guess. Your favorite book is *Hunt for Red October.*"

"No." He had a way of tilting his head and looking up at her from under his lashes when he was teasing. "That's my favorite movie."

"What is your favorite book?"

"I have two. *Lord of the Rings* and *Catch-22.*"

"What is it with men and war?"

"I bet you've never read either of those books if that's what you think."

"I've read *Lord of the Rings*."

He leaned forward. "You've never read *Catch-22*? Seriously? One of the great novels of our time."

"I've always meant to. I simply never did."

"There was always a juicy romance to be devoured instead."

She crossed her arms in front of her chest, the way her mother used to do when she was about to lecture. "And you've read Jane Austen's classic, have you?"

"That is not a manly read."

"Maybe you should read it before you judge."

"I'll read yours if you read mine," he teased.

She laughed. What she really had time for right now was another book to read that she hadn't chosen. But she nodded. "Sure."

He poured more sangria. "And your fiancé? Is he in LA, too?"

She felt heat crawl up the back of her neck. And for one second she was tempted to tell Dylan the truth. She glanced up and thought that even if he decided she was both a prevaricator and unhinged it was better than her continuing her foolish lie. At that moment the waiter arrived with her empanadas.

In the placing of dishes and asking if they needed anything else, the moment was lost. Instead of answering Dylan's question, she said, "What about you? What's your story?"

If he was aware that she'd sidestepped his question, he let it go.

He said, "My story is not so interesting either. My mom was a pretty famous model in the seventies and eighties. My dad was a photographer, that's how they met. But, I don't know, maybe the temptation of photographing beautiful women all day got to be too much for him. Anyway, he left us when I was little. He followed some young model to Paris, and he pretty much went from model to model until he died a couple of years ago."

"I'm sorry," she said.

He shrugged. "Truth is, I barely knew him."

"Your mom seems like an amazing woman."

"Oh, she is. When her modeling career was going well she put money away instead of blowing it. She loves vintage stores and she has a good eye. So she and her sister started Joe's."

"How do you like working in the vintage clothing business?"

"I like it fine. But I'm like you, waiting for my big break."

"There's a big break in vintage clothing?"

He settled back in his chair. "No. I've got a degree in business and I'm working on a startup company with some guys I met at college. At this point, it's nothing but hard work and hopes and dreams. But if it goes, it could be big."

"Wow, that's exciting. What kind of startup?"

"Internet security, that's all I can say. We all signed a non-disclosure."

"That sounds really exciting. In a sort of secret agent way."

"I think so. And, in the meantime, working at Joe's gives me a paycheck and when it's not busy, I work on my own stuff."

Even though the food was delicious, she barely tasted it. All her senses were busy enjoying Dylan's presence.

"Do you live above the store?" she asked. She'd noticed there was a full apartment there.

"No. It's mostly storage. My aunt sometimes stays there when she wants to spend the night in town. She's in Paris right now. She'll bring home some amazing vintage pieces and end up keeping most of them for herself."

She laughed. "Not the business head in the family."

He hesitated and she thought he was about to say more, but he only said, "No. But she loves her life, and I respect that."

"Where do you live?"

"I rent an apartment a few blocks away."

She fiddled with her plate. "Do you live alone?"

"I do. How about you?"

"I live near here, too. In the main floor suite of an old house." And, because she didn't want him thinking her boyfriend was part of her living arrangements she said, "My roommate writes a blog about being single in LA. She's also an actress and a writer, so it's never dull."

When they'd finished dinner, he walked her back to the store. She had left her car in a lot nearby. "Thank you," she said. "Tonight was . . . Magical."

He looked at her and said, "I wish . . ." He closed his eyes and then shook his head. "If you decide you want that dress, we'll do everything we can to make it work for you."

"Dylan . . ." No, she'd rather he thought she was engaged to another man than that she was so feeble she'd lied about being engaged so she could try on a wedding dress she couldn't even afford.

He'd turned and was waiting for her to continue. She said, "Let me know how you like *Pride and Prejudice*."

# CHAPTER 5

*W*hen Meg arrived home, she found June flopped on the couch watching television while simultaneously working on her laptop.

She glanced up when Meg walked in looking peevish. Meg said, "You're home already? How was the date with the professional athlete?" For all her cynicism, June was actively looking for Mr. Right, and Meg always hoped that on one of these dates she would find him. June scowled. "Professional athlete? He's a professional bowler. How is that even a sport?"

"Oh. Well, he could still be a very interesting person."

June glared at her from over the back of the couch. "Did I mention he bowls for a living?"

"I'm sorry."

"And look at you." She squinted her eyes with suspicion. "You seem pretty excited for a woman who went to a boring work thing."

Meg walked over and flopped besides her on the couch. "I need to tell you something." She could not keep all this to herself any longer. And, while June could sometimes be a challenging roommate, they were friends and no one knew the dating scene in LA better. She said, "I met someone."

"Oh, my God. Really? Where? How? When?"

"This is going to sound crazy. But I met him in a vintage clothing store."

"Not one of the top ten meeting spots in LA, but that's what's so great about this town. You never know when something incredible is going to happen." She flipped off the television so Meg knew she had her roommate's full attention. June leaned forward, excited. "Tell me everything."

And so she did. From the moment that dress had called to her to the moment she'd walked away from Dylan tonight.

June stared at her like she was crazy, and she could understand why.

"So, you met the dreamiest guy ever, told him you're engaged to another man, even though you haven't had a boyfriend in, what, two years? And you think there's hope for this relationship?"

In a strange way she did. Maybe she was just a crazed, over-read, under-sexed romantic, but when Dylan had gazed into her eyes, right from the first moment, she'd felt something magical happen.

"Yes. I do think there could be something there. He didn't have to extend the evening by asking me for dinner."

"Where did he take you?"

"An Argentinian place. Crowded and trendy."

"Good. I'm getting a definite dating vibe. But it was casual enough he could not be accused of being a skeevy douche trying to steal another man's fiancée."

"Exactly." She began to feel hopeful.

"Who paid?" June asked.

"He did, but he said the store was paying."

June nodded. "Again, it's a date without being an official date. He walked a fine line and he did it with style."

Even though she barely knew Dylan, she was proud of him for impressing June, who always looked for the dark side of men's behavior.

"So, when are you seeing him again?"

And wasn't that the question of the moment. "I don't know. It's not like we could make plans to meet again. I'm supposed to be engaged."

"Yes. That is the first thing you need to deal with." June settled herself more comfortably against the cushions. Meg looked at her hopefully—she was the in-house dating expert after all. She said, "I think this calls for ice cream."

"Chocolate?"

"Even better. I stocked up on rocky road on my way home from bowling boy."

"Excellent."

So, with bowls of ice cream on their laps, they strategized.

"What, exactly, have you told him about your supposed fiancé?" June asked.

"As little as I possibly could. He asked if my husband-to-be lived in LA and I managed to change the subject. I don't think I've told him a single thing."

"Good. Good." June scooped up some ice cream. "We need to get rid of the fiancé."

Meg nodded. She'd figured out this much herself.

June mulled over the issue for a moment. "Tell Dylan your guy is dead."

She swallowed a freezing cold lump of ice cream too fast and coughed. "Dead? You want me to kill off my own fiancé?"

"Sure. People die every day."

"That's a little harsh."

"I guess. Plus, there's the whole funeral thing. A fake fiancé is bad enough, but a fake funeral is kind of sketchy."

They ate more ice cream.

"Tell him you broke up, or better yet, your fake fiancé dumped you. That gets you the sympathy card."

"I don't want the man I'm interested in to think my fiancé dumped me right before the wedding. How would *that* make me look?"

"It would make you look pathetic." She waved her spoon around and a marshmallow wobbled alarmingly. "Well, then you broke up with him."

She didn't like this option either. "Doesn't that make me seem kind of faithless, like a woman you can't really count on?"

June leaned forward, pinning her with a fierce gaze. "You're going to have to kill him or dump him. You'd better make up your mind."

"What reason would I give for dumping him?"

"He cheated on you."

"Now we're back to me being pathetic."

"Good point. What if you said it's because you met someone else?"

"And let him know that he's that person?" It seemed too emotionally revealing. She was no good at cool, sophisticated banter that worked on two levels. She adored it on the movie screen or inside the pages of a novel. There was a reason she spent so much of her time inside books. "I don't know."

"Maybe he had to move away? And you love your job and you have a great apartment with the world's best roommate and you were not willing to relocate to Winnipeg."

"Winnipeg?"

"That's where bowling boy is from. Do you know it's winter there nine months of the year? And in the summer they have mosquitoes bigger than B-52s?"

"Could he have been exaggerating?"

"Exaggeration is only inflating the truth."

She contemplated this plan. "The man I planned to marry is

moving to Winnipeg and I don't want to follow him because the winters are too cold."

"Yes. It's logical and makes you sound in charge of your life and not pathetic." Pleased with her solution, June picked up the remote ready to flip the TV back on.

"If I loved someone, I'd followed him anywhere." She imagined that if Dylan moved to Winnipeg or Siberia she'd pack a bag with a down jacket and a lot of woolen underwear and go along with him if he asked her to. She banged her head against the soft back of the couch. "I never ever should've done such a stupid thing as pretend to be engaged in the first place."

"Well that's a given. But, now you're in this mess, we have to dig you out of it."

Meg put her empty bowl down on the table where it made a click of determination. "No. I am not telling any more lies, half lies, or white lies. I am going to go into Joe's Past and Present and tell him the truth."

"He's going to think you're deranged. You know that, right?"

She took in a deep breath. "I would rather he thinks I'm deranged than a liar."

June didn't seem so sure. "I think you should sleep on it."

But, of course, she barely slept. Their dinner out hadn't even been a real date and she'd had more fun than on any evening out with a man she could ever remember. Her last boyfriend had been a struggling writer. And, while it had been fascinating to be even peripherally involved in his creative process, they had spent most of their time either talking about his work, parsing rejection letters from editors for clues, or researching agents. Or she'd been editing his words. Now that she looked back, she'd discovered in herself a talent for editing.

In truth, he hadn't been a very good writer. He hadn't been a good boyfriend either. He was needy and self-absorbed and what she had imagined was his devotion to her was really insecurity.

She couldn't go on dreaming about Dylan all the time and then find out he despised her for lying. Anyway, she didn't even know if he was single. He'd said he lived alone, but that didn't mean he was unattached.

She spent Sunday shopping for groceries, doing errands and wondering if she'd hear from Dylan. She didn't, but why would she? The man believed she was engaged.

Monday morning she rose with determination. Whatever happened, she was going to make things right. She dressed with more than her usual care the next morning. A lot more. She let her hair hang in loose curls around her shoulders, put a lot more effort into her makeup, even following Nikki's suggestion that she do more with her eyes. She wore her best black skirt, black stockings and ankle boots, and a butterfly-patterned silk top.

When she got to the office and dumped out the paper manuscripts and placed them in a pile to be mailed back, her boss came into the small cubicle that was her office. His name was Anthony Rowan, and while all his clients loved him, she wasn't aware of a single person on staff here at RGW Entertainment who didn't pretty much hate his guts. She tried not to hate anyone, but Anthony could be challenging.

He motioned to the stack of paper with his chin. "Anything in there? *War and Peace? The Fault in Our Stars? Fifty Shades?*"

"Pale imitations of all those books, but nothing I'd want you to look at."

"Damn. We need a big hit, all our jobs depend upon it." He leaned over her desk. "I am counting on you."

As a motivational speech, it had worked the first time. Probably had a lot of impact the second time. But now, she heard this same speech pretty much every Monday morning. She replied, "I'll do my best."

Then she set to work. She contemplated going in to talk to Dylan on her lunch break, but she never got a lunch break. One of the Hollywood studios expressed interest in a book by one of their authors, and there went her day.

She left work a little early, justifying her departure with the fact that she'd skipped lunch altogether and that she wanted to get through six manuscripts tonight. When she got to Joe's Past and Present, her steps slowed and then stopped altogether. In the window, where that beautiful wedding dress should float, teasing her with the promise of a golden future, stood a naked mannequin. It looked so sad with its naked beige limbs that she wanted to throw a blanket over the poor thing. Then the most likely reason for its naked state struck her.

"No," she whispered. Panic beat at her breast. Surely they hadn't sold that dress already?

With an impending sense of urgency and doom, she pushed her way into the store. She had no idea who was currently trying on the dress, but they weren't getting it. That dress was hers. If she had to get into a bidding war, she would. Mentally, she catalogued all her assets and her savings. She'd been saving for a trip to Europe. She supposed she could raid that fund—and her rainy day fund in case she lost her job. If she did all that, plus maxed her credit card, she had a shot.

She could hear Dylan's voice. She paused behind a rack of prom gowns to listen. And what she heard amazed her. "It is a great dress," he said, sounding way less enthusiastic than when she'd tried it on. "Too bad it doesn't fit."

A female voice replied. "I absolutely love it." She could tell the voice was coming from the triple mirrors, so she peeked out. The woman in the dress was all wrong for it. She was too tall, too blonde, and way too skinny. Dylan was right. It didn't fit her at all. The dress was both too big in the body and too short. She wanted to run forward and snatch it off that skinny bone-rack. Instead, she stood there, rooted to the spot, recalculating her finances.

The woman twirled, and maybe it was her imagination, but

she didn't even think the dress twirled properly on that broomstick body. The young woman put a hand to her chest and the flash of a big, sparkly engagement ring nearly blinded all of them.

She said, "I can have it altered. I love it. I'll take it."

Just as Meg was about to scream, "No!" and leap out from behind the prom dresses, Dylan said, "I'm sorry. That dress is on hold for someone else."

The woman's eyes opened wide. "But I want it."

"I'll tell you what we'll do, if the woman who has it on hold doesn't take it, you'll be the first one I call."

She didn't miss the simpering grin. "Why don't we pretend the dress isn't on hold? I will pay full price and take it today. I could even run to the bank and get you cash."

"I'm sorry," Dylan said, quite firmly. "Store policy is that the person who puts a garment on hold has first dibs."

Her face fell. "Well, when will you know for sure?"

"The end of the week. But I should warn you, she seemed very definite."

"But it looked so fantastic on your website. That's why I came in. I saw that dress and I knew I had to have it."

He nodded. "There's been a lot of interest."

Now she realized she had more competition than the skinny blonde. Who had put this gown on hold? And why did she have this spooky feeling, growing stronger by the second, that the gown had to be hers?

Slowly, carefully, and quietly she backed out of the store, easing open the door so the bell wouldn't tinkle too loudly.

She had to figure out a way to buy that dress. It was insane, of course. She needed a wedding dress like she needed braces on her straight teeth, but the crazy notion wouldn't leave her.

A different person might have taken their personal torment into a bar and ordered straight whisky and then bored the bartender with their problems. For Meg, her place of refuge was a bookstore.

She walked, and she kept walking. She came to a secondhand bookstore, one of her favorites. It stocked everything from old classics to out-of-print cookbooks and last month's category romances. She headed in. She even loved the smell of the old paper. A fluffy orange cat sat on a pillow on the top shelf of the philosophy section and stared sleepily down at her. She wandered the squished aisles, peering at mythology, sleep disorders and Russian fiction, and all the ideas and stories packed into the space soothed her.

An entire sci-fi and fantasy section suggested other worlds existed, the crime and mystery shelves promised that evil would be punished and order restored, and in the romance section, ordinary girls were swept off their feet by billionaires.

If all these stories were possible, then how hard could it be for one determined woman to buy a second hand wedding dress?

But, if she bought the dress, it would effectively end her relationship with Dylan. He'd believe she was going to wear it down the aisle to marry her invented fiancé, and, instead, the dress would hang in her closet reminding her of the man she'd fallen for.

On the other hand, if she didn't buy the dress, and soon, some other bride would and then she felt the spell would be broken. While she was wandering, she found three copies of *Catch-22*. She chose the one with the clearest print, paid for the book and tucked it in her bag, and headed home.

Maybe she hadn't ever read the book, but she knew what a catch-22 was. And she was in a good one.

# CHAPTER 6

"I have to hand it to you, Dylan," Joe said once the afternoon rush had cleared out. "The advertising we did is really paying off. We've already sold four of those bridesmaid dresses and sales in general are way up. I'm really surprised that we haven't sold the Evangeline wedding dress."

Dylan had no idea what he was doing. He had talked three women out of that dress, three women who were willing to pay five grand. But something in him couldn't let that dress go. When he had seen Meg wearing the gown, and then, even worse, Joe had made him act like he was her bridegroom and he'd slipped a wedding ring onto her finger, well, he wasn't the most romantic guy in the world but something profound and irreversible had happened to him.

He was a practical man, a guy with a business degree who worried about Internet security. He wasn't a fall-in-love-at-first-sight-with-a-stranger kind of person. And yet, that's exactly what had happened to him. He'd fallen hard and fast for a pair of brown eyes and a shy smile. Worse, he'd fallen for a woman he couldn't have.

Trust him. If he had to suddenly discover love at first sight, couldn't he have at least found a woman who was available?

He said, "I know. It hasn't been quite right for anyone but Meg." Since his mother was now working with him in the store he figured he'd better make it clear to her that the dress was not for sale. He said, "I know we don't normally do this, but I put the gown on hold for her."

She raised her eyebrows. "No. We don't usually do that. I think it was you who told me that it was bad business."

"I did. But, think about it. As soon as the Evangeline gown is gone, our business drops back to what it was. It's not like we have a string of Evangeline designer gowns and we can pull another one from the back stockroom. I think it's smart business to keep the dress in stock at least for a couple of weeks."

"A couple of weeks? Is that how long she wants the dress on hold for?"

"I think she's waiting for a paycheck." What was he doing? He hadn't lied to his mother since he was a rebellious teen.

And there was the reason he never lied to his mother. Because she could see right through him. She looked at him now and her face wrinkled with concern. "What are you doing?"

He shook his head. "I don't know. If I figure it out, you'll be the first to know."

"That girl is engaged. That means she is going to marry another man."

"I know."

"Anyway, aren't you still seeing Amy?"

"No." Amy had been his girlfriend at Stanford. When he'd moved to LA after graduating, she'd moved to San Jose to work for one of the big Internet firms. They'd kept up for a while, but since he hadn't bothered to see her in the last couple of months, and she hadn't tried to see him, he figured they were done. His mother had never liked her anyway. "You should be happy I'm not with Amy anymore."

"I am happy you're not with Amy anymore. I just don't want you to get your heart broken by some girl who is not available."

"Don't worry about me."

"It's what mothers do."

He couldn't argue with that. "I'm heading out to get some lunch. Can I pick you up anything?"

"No. I'll get something later."

He went to one of his favorite lunch spots. They made great sandwiches, excellent coffee, and offered free Wi-Fi. He pulled out his laptop. He decided to check on the online advertising they had done and to see if a press release he'd sent out had been picked up by any bloggers. He was munching and scrolling when he came across a blog post. The title was, "No, your Big Balls aren't enough."

He had no idea why he clicked through to the blog post but he found himself reading about the trials of a single woman dating in LA who called herself Single Chick in LA. The big balls referred to the professional athlete she had met online who turned out to be a professional bowler. From Winnipeg. He found the article to be funny and edgy. He liked single chick's style so he scrolled through to her home page, which featured an even newer post. He nearly choked on his sandwich.

"She finally meets a great guy, then lies and tells him she's engaged."

This woman, LA Single Chick, told the horrifying story about how her roommate, a woman who tended to spend most nights at home with a good book, had met an amazing guy and been so flustered she told him she was engaged.

He recalled Meg's words while they were having dinner. "My roommate blogs about being a single girl in LA." No doubt there were hundreds of blogs about dating in LA, possibly thousands for all he knew. He read the entire article. Then he read the comments. There were fifty-nine of them. People encouraging this girl to do everything from get out more, to tell the guy the truth. One comment warned that he probably liked her because she was unavailable. "It sucks sweaty donkey, but the truth is, your LA guy will be crazy about you when he can't have you, then forget you exist when you make yourself available."

He slapped down his urge to rebut that comment. He knew there were a lot of bitter women out there, but a man did not stay single so he could mess with nice women's heads. Sometimes, men got screwed over by love too.

He knew he was reading a lot into a random blog post, but something had been off about Meg and her wedding from the first time she'd walked into Joe's and asked about the dress. She wore no engagement ring. When he'd asked if they'd set a date, she'd looked flustered and said they hadn't. He asked if she was seeing her guy on Saturday night and she'd said he was out of town. He remembered asking if her fiancé lived in LA and, now he came to think of it, she hadn't replied.

He sipped coffee and gave the matter some thought. There was no way an intelligent woman like Meg would not notice that he was completely smitten with her. So why hadn't she told him the truth? He could understand that a woman who was in a store trying on a wedding dress would say she was engaged. Of course she would. Because who would do such a thing? Who would try on a wedding gown if she wasn't engaged?

Then he thought about his own behavior and had to question why a man would organize an advertising campaign just to get to see a woman again, a woman who was not free.

He was used to things that made sense. Business was pretty clear. It acquired inventory, or created a service, offered it for sale. People bought it or they didn't. A business operated on profits and losses, inventory, salaries, and a score of other factors that were quantifiable.

But dating? Relationships between men and women? They were complicated, and one sex didn't make sense to the other half the time. His own actions made no sense, and he considered himself a sensible, down-to-earth man. He went back and read the blog post one more time. Then he skimmed back and read random posts from the past few months. The roommate didn't get mentioned a whole lot, but he got a picture of a quiet, shy person who preferred books to parties. There was a hilarious post where single chick had tried to convince the shy friend to go on an Internet double date.

Maybe he was crazy and plenty of women lied about being engaged and had roommates who blogged about it. But he began to feel more hopeful than he'd felt in days.

What if Meg wasn't engaged after all?

He put away his laptop and pulled out the well-thumbed copy of *Pride and Prejudice* that he'd found on his mother's bookshelf.

He opened the book and read the first page. Women scheming to marry rich men. Oh, good. Exactly his kind of story. He could sit and read Single Chick in LA and get the same story—some things never changed. He yawned, checked the time, and decided he'd give Jane Austen exactly fifteen minutes.

To his surprise, he caught himself chuckling by page three. Maybe there was more to this novel than the bagging of rich dudes by poor women.

~

WHEN HE RETURNED to Joe's after lunch, he found his mother packing yet another of the bridesmaid dresses. Two other customers waited in line to pay.

He immediately went to help. He bagged purchases and joked with the customers, until the rush was over and there were only two women flicking through garments in a way that suggested they were merely browsing.

"You're in a better mood since you got back from lunch."

"Low blood sugar," he said.

"Since when do you suffer from low blood sugar?"

"Just be glad I'm happy."

"I am. Oh, and Janet's back. That should make you even happier."

"When did she get in? And what did she bring with her? Or, should I say, has she brought anything for the store?"

Janet was his aunt and the co-owner of Joe's. She was by nature a wanderer. She'd financed her travels by writing about her experiences, many of them humorous accounts of her adventures as a single woman of a certain age. To her surprise as much as anyone's, she had become famous and quite rich. Janet also loved pretty things. When she and Joe had decided to open the store, she'd decreed that she would be their international buyer. Although she did bring some choice items to the vintage store, most of her shopping ended up in her own closet.

Joe headed out later to attend an antique auction with several lots of vintage clothing. Things were quiet enough while she was gone that he was able to spend an hour going over the marketing plan for their Internet startup. He wasn't one of the software engineers on the project. His flair was for the practicalities of business. Any fool could see the screaming need for better Internet privacy and security. And his firm was by no means the only one working on the problem. When they launched, marketing would be critical.

The jingle of the bell made him look up. A young Asian-American woman walked in. She wore a short black dress with black high heels and had the solid build of an athlete.

She didn't browse through the store at all, but walked straight up to him. "Hi. I'd like to try on the wedding dress in the window."

He was getting tired of dragging that dress in and out of the display. He looked her up and down. "It's not going to fit you."

Her eyes widened in surprise. "How do you know?"

He didn't want to sound rude by making comments about her figure, so he said, "It's made for a much taller woman."

She gave him a scornful glance. "I can have it turned up."

He could sense that she was not going to be fobbed off. So, once more, he climbed up into the window and carefully removed the dress from the mannequin. "Anyway," she said, "it's not for me. It's for a friend."

"Why doesn't she come in and try it on herself?"

She stepped closer, close enough that her shoulder rubbed his arm. "Morning sickness. She doesn't want to throw up on the dress. She saw it on your website and really wanted it."

He didn't entirely believe the story, and worse, he was pretty sure this woman was hitting on him. It happened sometimes; he was the only guy in a store with a lot of female traffic.

He set her up in the fitting room and left her to it. In a few minutes she waltzed out, holding the bodice up to her chest. She blinked her lashes at him. "Could you do me up at the back?"

He glanced around, but of course Joe wasn't back yet. "Sure."

As he'd already told her, the dress was entirely the wrong size. He did up two buttons at her waist but to do any more would strain the material. He said, "Take a look in the mirror."

She didn't seem to mind that most of her back was exposed. If anything, he thought she was teasing him with as much skin as she could get away with. She was pretty and kind of funny and if he wasn't already hugely into another woman, he'd have flirted back. But he had no interest in other women right now. After she studied the dress from every angle she said, "I think I'll buy it for her. Do you take credit cards?"

"You're a very generous friend." He lifted the trailing skirt so she wouldn't trip over it. "Do you know how much this dress costs?"

"No. I guess I should've asked that."

"It's five grand."

She didn't seem very surprised. "Well, I'll take it anyway."

"I'm sorry. It's really not for sale."

She eyed him with deep suspicion. "You just told me it's five grand."

"I know. And we will sell it eventually. We're hanging onto it for inventory purposes."

"Inventory? Isn't the whole idea of having a store to get rid of inventory?"

"You're right. Normally. But, this is such a special gown, that we want to hang onto it for a while."

"When do you think it might be available?"

"Probably not before your friend starts showing."

She sidled up to him one more time. She tossed her long, black hair over her shoulder and gazed up at him. "Why don't I take you out for a drink and you can explain to me exactly what I would have to do to get you to sell me this dress."

He grinned at her. He couldn't help it. She was a woman who knew what she wanted and went for it. Also, he liked how upfront she was. He said, "I'd like to, but I can't."

"Why not? Are you seeing someone?"

If she could be honest and direct, he supposed he could too. He said, "I'm working on it."

"Well, it's a beautiful dress. Some lucky bride's going to look like a princess in it."

"We have an entire bridal section over there. Maybe there's something there that would suit your friend?"

"I don't think so. She's a woman who knows exactly what she wants." Then she went back into the changing room and put herself back into her street clothes. When she left, he returned the gown once more to the front window, resisting the urge to plant a SOLD sign on it.

# CHAPTER 7

"*You* did *what?*" Meg stared at June, so horrified her scalp tingled with humiliation.

"I was testing your theory," June explained. "Is the Evangeline dress for sale or isn't it? And if it was on hold, I was going to try and find out who it was on hold for."

"So you went into the vintage store without telling me you were going, and got Dylan to let you try on *my* wedding dress?"

"It's not your wedding dress because you haven't bought it yet. Anyway, you're going to like what I have to say."

Somehow Meg doubted it. But she had to know. "Okay, tell me everything. Every single detail and every word you both spoke."

"Deal. First, you have excellent taste. Your guy's friggin' gorgeous."

She knew that, but it was still nice to have her taste confirmed.

"So I said I wanted to try on the dress and he looked at me and said it wouldn't fit."

Meg couldn't help but chuckle at the indignation in her friend's tone. "He was probably right. You're a lot more muscular than I am." Also, several inches shorter, but she didn't point that out.

"Then I said it wasn't for me, it was for my friend. And then he wanted to know why my friend wasn't there, so I said she was pregnant."

"You said you were buying a wedding dress for a pregnant lady?"

"I was explaining to him why I, a single woman, might want to try on a wedding gown."

Meg didn't like the spurt of jealousy she experienced when she thought of June making it very clear to Dylan that she was a single woman. "So, did he let you try it on?"

"Of course he did. I'm very persuasive. And, he was right, it didn't fit it all. So I hit on him."

"You did not!" She felt the same way about Dylan that she did about the gown. She didn't want other women touching him.

"Chica, it was the best way to find out if he was available."

"You hit on him how exactly?"

"First, I let him know with some subtle body language that I was interested. And then I asked him out for a drink."

"Wow. Subtlety is your middle name."

"Don't worry. He turned me down."

A little butterfly of hope danced around in her belly. "He turned you down?"

"Yep, and I asked him why. I asked if he was seeing someone."

Even though she hated that June had gone behind her back and blundered into Dylan's store and got herself involved in Meg's possible love life, she was still dying to hear everything that had happened. "And what did he say?"

"He said he's working on it."

"What do you think that means? Could he be referring to

me?" Or more likely there was another woman he was interested in.

"I don't know. But here's the cool thing. I told him I wanted to buy the dress for my friend and he wouldn't let me."

"You were going to buy it?" What on earth would June do with an expensive wedding gown? And where would she get five grand?

"No, of course I wasn't. I'd have said I changed my mind before I actually bought it. But here's the thing. He didn't tell me the dress was on hold for someone else. He said they want to keep it on display for some bogus inventory thing. It was completely lame. And obviously not true. But he absolutely did not want me to have that dress."

"That is interesting. What do you think it means?"

"Hey, I'm just the field cop. You're the detective."

"Why do relationships have to be so complicated?"

June stared at her. "This would be the simplest relationship in the history of male-female relationships if you hadn't started out by telling the man that you are engaged. And now you're too much of a weenie to tell him you're not."

Meg dropped her head in her hands. "You're right."

"I know you. It's because you're afraid of rejection. So long as you can have this non-relationship that's all teasy in promise and no action, because you're engaged to another man, you don't have to face the possibility that he will reject you."

She didn't have the strength to argue. "Or I might find out that he's not even interested."

"And you think online dating is difficult."

"Online dating *is* difficult," she wailed. "All dating is difficult."

"You said it, girl." June wore running gear, and her hair was tied back in a ponytail. She said, "I'm heading out for a run. Tell you what, why don't I pick up sushi on my way home?"

It was one of their favorite indulgences. And right now, Meg felt as though she needed a small indulgence. She had no time to cook, not with the pressing need to find a great project, a great manuscript, or a great client to bring to the firm. She didn't want to remain an assistant for very much longer. She thought, if she had to keep slaving away to Anthony Rowan, she would be putting his life in danger.

"Do you have a date tonight?" It was rare that June didn't have either a date or an audition.

"No," she said. "I'm working at home tonight."

Meg felt slightly alarmed. If June was rehearsing for a part, she would want her roommate to run her lines with her. And Meg simply didn't have the time. Her expression must been pretty transparent for June grinned at her. "Don't worry. I'll be as quiet in my room as you are in yours."

Oh good, this week she was a serious writer. Meg liked her roommate both ways, but it was definitely more peaceful when she was a struggling writer than when she was a struggling actress. "You got over your writer's block?"

June tossed her ponytail. "You were right. All I needed to do was sit down and really think about what my character wanted. We did an interview and she told me. It was pretty cool."

"Excellent."

"I don't know if it's so excellent, but at least I'm getting words on paper."

"That's how most writers do it."

"There should be an easier way."

DYLAN CLOSED up the store as he walked by he sent a glance to the gown hovering in the window. He felt that since that dress had appeared in his life, everything seemed to have changed. Before that, he'd been all about work. Now, he was having trouble concentrating. He had a bad case of unrequited love.

He played hockey on Wednesday nights. It was a ragtag group and they weren't very good, but then neither was most of the competition in their league. But he liked the guys, and the cold, clean feel of his skates scraping the ice in the single-minded determination it took to attempt to figure out, as Wayne Gretzky had so famously said, not where the puck was, but where it was going to be. He was never going to be a Gretzky. In fact, he liked the quote more for its application to business than to sport.

That's what his startup was attempting to do. Find solutions not for today, but for two, five, and ten years down the road. Security and privacy were big issues now, but it was only going to get worse.

After hockey, he and some of the other players went out for a burger. And then he headed home thinking he had to be the ultimate New Age guy to spend one part of his evening crushing other players into the boards in a hockey arena and then finish his evening settled on the couch reading *Pride and Prejudice.*

But he never did get to Jane Austen. His mom called and said, "Janet is over here now. Why don't you stop by and say hello to her. And check out what she brought for us."

"Sounds good," he said, and changed direction.

His mother, who did not run vintage stores because she needed the money, but really to give her something to do all day, lived in Hancock Park in a house built in the 1920s. When he walked in, he could hear the two women laughing and talking, against the backdrop of Sam Smith crooning in the background. He walked back to the kitchen, where the noise was coming from, and found the two of them sharing a bottle of wine in the den beside the kitchen. Janet was in a twenties phase and fit right in with the architecture.

The garments draped and spilled over the couches looked like the wardrobe from *Downton Abbey* after World War I. There were silks, slim lined flapper dresses, exquisite nightgowns, hats, bags, and even shoes.

Janet got up when she saw him and pulled him in for a scented hug.

You would know these two were sisters anywhere. They both shared the same huge dark eyes, and the dark hair. His mother still wore hers long and let it streak with silver, while his aunt had hers cropped in a style that went very well with the clothing strewn all over the room. In his opinion, she wasn't as pretty as his mother, but she was still a striking woman.

"And don't you get better looking every time I see you?" His aunt said, twinkling up at him.

Since she said this pretty much every time she saw him, he had long ago ceased to be embarrassed by her words. He said, "How was Paris? I can see that the shopping was good."

"Oh, these are the dresses I bought just for me. But wait until you see what I got for the store."

He glanced at his mother and she shrugged. He suspected that this was the cream of the purchases.

"I was telling Joe, I think I met someone."

"Janet was fifty-five years old and had buried one husband and divorced two. She still enjoyed an active social life, and more than that he really didn't want to know.

He liked his aunt; she was sophisticated, funny, and he probably couldn't name a place she hadn't visited, or at least tried to visit. She wasn't a travel writer who got free trips and then wrote puff pieces. She traveled on her own dime and never shied away from saying what she thought. But, as much as her books were about new places and experiences, they were as much about her comic view of the world.

He settled on the couch and heard about Francois who ran a winery. He suspected Francois would end up in the next travelogue but that Janet wasn't serious enough about him that there'd be a fourth wedding anytime soon.

Still, it was nice to catch up and hear about her travels. "I need to start writing my next book to pay for it all," she sighed.

"And finance your next trip."

She twinkled at him. "And that. Peru's calling I think. Or maybe Russia." They spent a couple of hours talking, mostly about her trip, and then she showed the items she'd bought for Joe's Past and Present. As he'd expected, she'd kept the best for herself but there was still a pretty good haul to add to their stock.

As he was leaving, he noticed the usual fan of invitations on his mother's desk in the kitchen. Even though she hadn't modeled for a number of years, she was still very connected. She was always invited to parties, gallery openings, fashion galas. His eyes scanned idly over the many invitations and stopped at one. He picked up the card. The old Malvern Mansion was reopening as a restaurant. There was nothing new or interesting about this, restaurants opened and closed all the time in LA. This invitation offered the usual. Come, enjoy wine and hors d'oeuvres and check out the space. But what made him pause was that the mansion also offered wedding packages. He picked up the card and said to his mom, "Are you planning to go to this opening?"

She glanced over at him. "Which one is that, honey?"

"The Malvern Mansion. You're invited for cocktails and hors d'oeuvres. It's this Friday night."

His mother wrinkled her nose. "I've already got plans for Friday." Then she looked at him, puzzled. "Are you interested in going?"

"Yes." He racked his brain to think of a reason why a single twenty-eight-year-old man might want to check out an old mansion that was offering stuffy, overpriced meals and wedding packages. He came up with, "I thought our advertising campaign was really successful. Maybe we should do something similar, where we join with other businesses."

He motioned to Janet's collection of fabulous French vintage garments. "We could put something together that's period. Maybe join together with the mansion, a winery, a florist, and a jeweler in our advertising."

It was a crazy idea, but like many crazy ideas, he kind of liked it.

His aunt was equally enthusiastic. "That is a fantastic idea. I am always saying that we should spread our wings and be more a part of the business community in our area."

Joe looked at him with mild suspicion. "I think it's a great idea to go. Do you want to take my invitation? It's for two, so you could invite a guest."

"Yeah. I think I'll check it out."

"Let me know what you think of the food and wine list."

"I will."

He tucked the invitation into his pocket, said goodbye to the two sisters and headed out.

He felt that Meg was essentially an honest woman. He had an idea that he might offer to take her as his guest to check out this charming new wedding venue since she had already told him that she hadn't chosen a place to get married and have her reception.

Hopefully, she would admit that she was not actually engaged.

He called her as soon as he got home.

"Hello?" He loved the sound of her voice. It was soft, a little tentative, even though she must have call display and know who was calling.

He said, "I have an idea that I hope you like."

"Really? I'm listening."

"Remember you told me you did not have a wedding and reception venue chosen?"

There was a tiny pause. "Yes, I do remember telling you that."

"Have you found one?"

"No. Not yet."

"Great. I've been invited to the opening of the Malvern Mansion. Since they're newly reopened I bet you could get a screaming deal on a wedding package. And, even if you don't like the idea of getting married there, it might be fun to go to their opening on Friday night and sample their wines and their menu."

"This Friday night?"

"Yeah, sorry for the short notice. Are you busy?"

Once more, he heard hesitation. "No. I'm not busy. I'm not sure I want to get married in an old mansion though."

"Well, it doesn't hurt to check out a possible venue. You should have some comparisons."

"I guess."

"How about I pick you up Friday at seven?"

"That would be good."

He didn't want to end the call. He wanted to talk to her all night, and hear her soft voice. He said, "Are you still thinking about the wedding gown?"

"I rarely think of anything else," she said irritably.

He chuckled. "That's because it's your dress."

"I know. I'm going to figure something out."

"Good."

There was another pause and he said, "Did you find a copy of *Catch-22*?"

"I did. I can't say it's my favorite book of all time, but I can see the appeal."

"All I ask is an open mind."

"How about you? Have you dug into *Pride and Prejudice* yet?"

"As a matter of fact, I have. I thought I was going to hate the book, but it's funny. I think Mr. Collins's marriage proposal is one of the funniest scenes I've ever read."

She grew instantly enthusiastic. "I know! Honestly, I think

the three marriage proposals in the novel are three of the most brilliant scenes ever written."

"Three? I have to wade through three marriage proposals?"

"Trust me, you'll laugh, you'll cringe. I cried but you probably won't."

"Trust me, if I do, I am never telling you."

She was still laughing when the call ended.

"'m going to have to tell him," Meg said to June, as she related the phone conversation. "I don't even know why I said yes to Friday night."

June stared at her. "Of course you do. You're into him. You want to spend every second you can with him, and, he did kind of ask you for a date."

"Not exactly a date. He's helping me choose the wedding venue for a wedding to another man."

"Are you sure you can't just kill your fiancé off?"

"No, I'm not a murderer. Not even of a fictitious person that I made up in my head."

"Well, when this all goes south, don't come crying to me."

"Thank you for your support."

She spent all of Thursday stressing. When she wasn't stressing about what she was going to wear on Friday night she was stressing about what she was going to say, and how she was going to tell Dylan the truth. Because she was determined now that she had to tell him the truth.

When he arrived on Friday night at seven, exactly when he had said he would be there, she was all ready. June had two dates tonight. She was meeting another actor for drinks, and later on she was meeting a guy who made videos on YouTube. Meg only had one date this week and she was exhausted from thinking about it, she could not imagine how June kept up her busy social life.

She jumped into his car, an aging Honda, and thought how incredible he looked. Her heart jumped just being beside him.

He said, "Thanks for coming tonight. I have an idea about getting some advertising together with Joe's Past and Present and the mansion, and maybe a few other businesses. My aunt bought a collection home from Paris mostly from the 20s. We could do something Gatsby-ish."

"That's a great idea."

"If you want another modeling gig. It's yours."

"Thanks."

"My mother said you're a natural. If you keep modeling for us you'll have enough credits to get the Evangeline gown for free."

Oh that dress. They always came back to that dress.

When they arrived at the mansion she was surprised how many people Dylan knew. There were other restaurateurs, PR people, newspaper people, some influential bloggers, a couple of restaurant reviewers and the kind of beautiful people that made a venue sparkle. He said, "Usually it's my mom who comes to these things. But she was busy tonight so she gave me her tickets."

"I'm glad," she said. They wandered around from room to room and when he introduced her it was always as, "My friend Meg." She accepted a glass of wine from a passing tray and while they mingled and chatted she nibbled on various hors d'oeuvres. Everything tasted delicious, and when the owners came by in tuxedos to greet them, she was deeply relieved that Dylan did not present her as a possible bride who was checking out the venue. For that she was eternally grateful.

It was a beautiful evening and along with restored rooms from the turn-of-the-century mansion there were outdoor gardens, stone balconies and walled gardens that were lit up. It was magical. He led her out to a secluded spot on the stone balcony and as they looked over the lit gardens, he said, "What do you think? Is this a place you'd like to get married and have your reception?"

She turned to him. His eyes were dark and mysterious in the dim light and she thought her world would be perfect if it was this man she was marrying.

She said, "Dylan, there's something I really need to tell you. It's kind of embarrassing, really, but—"

"Why, Dylan! How wonderful to see you here."

He turned and she thought a glimmer of annoyance crossed his face. Her heart was still pounding and her lips were forming the words "I'm not engaged," but she didn't get a chance to speak them because a very elegant-looking woman who seemed kind of familiar came towards them. She wore a deep blue silk dress that looked like something out of the jazz age. Her hair was bobbed and she wore a long string of pearls.

"Janet," Dylan said, sounding a little acidic. "I had no idea you were coming here."

"You know how it is, I just got back from Paris," she said to Meg, nodding her head pleasantly. "And when I went through my invitations, this one caught my eye. I thought if I wore this vintage gown, people might ask where I got it, and I could tell them I'm one of the owners of Joe's Past and Present vintage store."

Now Meg realized why this woman had seemed familiar. She was clearly Joe's sister and Dylan's aunt. Before Dylan could introduce them, the woman held out her hand. "I'm Janet. Dylan's aunt."

She stuck to the same line Dylan had used all night. "Hi, I'm Meg. Dylan's friend."

"Oh, you are more than just friends." Her eyes widened. Could this woman see right through her? Did she read minds? Did she know that her feelings towards Dylan were not just friendly, but passionate? Before she could say a word, his aunt continued, "I recognize you from the photographs. You're the lovely model who showed off that Evangeline wedding gown so beautifully. Dylan, you have a very good eye."

She felt there was an undertone here and Dylan answered coolly, "I do, don't I?"

There was an awkward pause and she filled it by saying, "Paris? I would love to go there."

"It is a wonderful city. Crowded at this time of year, of course. But since I'm a travel writer as well as a vintage store co-owner I tend to get treated very well."

"You're a travel writer?"

"Yes. My writing name is Janet Delaney."

Meg's eyes opened wide once more. "Janet Delaney? Oh, my gosh. I love your books. You have the most wonderful way of making a person forget that they're reading a travel guide. It's like a friend is taking you through a city. Oh, that story about the pickpocket in Barcelona? I laughed so hard I cried."

They compared her to Bill Bryson. And Meg, who had been feeling anxiety for weeks as the principal agents in her company decided who was going to get the promotion to agent, suddenly felt that this woman had been planted in her path as a gift. If she could convince Dylan's aunt to bring her considerable business to their agency, she'd be a shoe in for the job. She said, "I'm a literary agent. If I could find another Janet Delaney, I would be very happy."

The woman laughed, a cool, delicious sound. "If there is another Janet Delaney, I'm going to have to find a new job." She took a sip of her champagne. "What agency do you work for?"

"RDW entertainment."

"That's a good firm. I'm with William Penniman and Associates in New York. They've been very good to me."

Damn. Damn, damn, damn. "Well, that's good to know." She knew the agency, of course, but didn't think they had a film agent. "Have they ever considered any of your projects for a movie?"

Janet's pearls swung as she shrugged. "People always talk about movies. Especially after *Under the Tuscan Sun* came out, and then *Eat, Pray, Love*. Suddenly travel memoir was all the rage. But nothing came of that."

"If I had a producer interested in doing something with one of your projects, would you be interested?"

"Honey, anything that makes me money has me interested."

Meg slipped one of her business cards out of her purse. She never went anywhere without them. She passed the card over. "I'd love to take you for lunch sometime and hear about your experiences. Honestly, you are one of my heroes."

Janet beamed. "Well, isn't she the sweetest thing."

"I think so," said Dylan.

"Well, children, I better go mingle and make nice. It was lovely to meet you, Meg."

"It was amazing to meet you."

After Janet went back inside, she turned to Dylan. "Oh, my gosh, I had no idea your aunt was Janet Delaney."

"We keep her privacy and leave it up to her who she tells. If she divulged her identity to you, it means she likes you. It was cool watching you work. Very smooth and ruthless. I think Henneman or Penniman or whoever her agent is better watch out."

"I am not ruthless, or smooth—what I am is desperate. If I could land even a piece of your aunt's business it could get me that promotion."

"You know I don't have any influence over her business."

"Of course." But her mind was spinning with possibilities.

"I think you were about to tell me something when my aunt interrupted us."

She was so glad they'd been interrupted before she admitted she'd lied. If Janet Delaney heard about that, she could kiss any hopes of the woman's business goodbye. Anyway, it was so nice to be here with Dylan and enjoy his company. Chances were, when he discovered she'd tried on that dress under false pretenses, he'd realize she was completely nuts and stay as far away from her as he could.

She said, "I think I was going to tell you that as much as I love this venue, I don't see myself getting married here."

He gazed at her and for a moment she thought she saw sadness cross his face. "Where do you see yourself getting married?"

"I think I'd want something simple. I'm not one of those people who wants a marriage commissioner to marry me on a beach, or a mountaintop. I want to get married in a real church. And have a reception afterwards. In a garden, maybe in a small restaurant. That's what I think I want."

He laughed. "For someone who's getting married soon, you should probably make up your mind about what you want."

Oh, she knew what she wanted. Her problem was she didn't know how she was going to get it.

MEG ASSUMED that Saturday was a busy day for Dylan. But, they seemed to be hanging out as friends, and, since he'd invited her to the opening of the old mansion, she thought she would reciprocate.

She stopped by, happy to see her dress still hanging in the window, and went in.

Joe, Janet, and Dylan were all visible. The two women ran

the till while Dylan was up on a ladder, fixing the rail that had fallen off one of the change rooms.

He looked happy to see her, glancing down to say, "Hey. You find the next Hemingway yet?"

She shook her head. Another Saturday morning wasted.

"I wondered if you wanted to see a movie premiere with me?"

He motioned her to hand him the curtain rod that was on the ground, resting on top of the red velvet curtain. "A movie premiere?"

She knelt down and hefted it up to him. "Yes. One of our projects was made into a movie, and since I was heavily involved in making it happen, I've got two tickets to the premier and the party afterwards. I thought it would be really nice to take a date. I get so tired of going to these things by myself."

Even as she realized that a woman who was engaged probably shouldn't be attending a lot of social functions by herself, he said, "Your fiancé doesn't like movies?"

"No. Plus, he travels a lot. We don't really spend much time together."

He hooked the curtain rod back into place. Gave the whole thing a tug and then climbed down the ladder.

"When is it?"

She told him. He pulled out his phone and made a note in his calendar. "Sure. I'd love to. Is it black tie or anything?"

"No. What you wore the other night would be perfect."

"Great." She didn't know what else to say, so she turned to browse when he said, "I was about to grab some lunch. Do you want to—" He stopped speaking and she thought a look of horror crossed his face. She turned and followed his gaze and saw a woman who was probably a couple of years older than her walk forward. She had dark hair and smart-girl glasses and a beautiful mouth highlighted with red lipstick. She wore designer jeans, a blouse that looked as though it cost more than

Meg's annual salary, and her green Kelly bag was probably not a knock off.

She had a look about her, both entitled and sure of herself, that made Meg feel that she was either from a very rich background or on the fast track in some profession, or maybe both. She returned Meg's regard with raised eyebrows. And, while Meg watched as though a terrible accident were happening in front of her and she was powerless to stop it, the woman walked right up to Dylan and kissed him full on the mouth.

"Amy," he said. "What are you doing here?"

She laughed, then slipped her arm around him. To Meg, she said, "He's such a tease. I'm his girlfriend. Where else would I be?"

Meg didn't even know what to say. She'd never been good at awkward social situations. Her instinct was always either to babble something inane or to run away. She was too shocked to babble anything inane, so she went with her default option. "Thanks for helping me out with that dress," she said to Dylan. "Better be going."

"Meg, wait . . ." But she was already heading for the door as fast as she could.

# CHAPTER 9

"*M*eg!" Dylan stared after the retreating figure, willing her not to open the door and walk out. But she did. Without so much as turning around. He took a step forward to go after her but Amy clamped a hand around his arm.

"Dylan. Don't."

He was beyond frustrated. He turned to her. "Why are you here?"

Amy was always so sure of herself, so directed. She knew what she wanted, figured out how to get it, and worked with single-minded purpose to achieve her goals. He had always admired that about her. However, he had the uncomfortable suspicion that for some reason she had decided that maybe, after two months of silence, she wanted him after all.

She licked her full lips. He knew it wasn't a sexy gesture, it was something she did when she was nervous. She said, "Is there somewhere we could go and talk?"

He glanced around. The store wasn't super busy and he had planned to go to lunch. He felt that he and Amy should resolve things between them once and for all so he said, "Sure. There's a coffee shop around the corner."

He walked up to his mother. "Okay if I head out for half an hour?"

She glanced at Amy. "Hello, Amy."

"Hello."

The greetings were cool. These two had never liked each other. "Of course. Take all the time you need."

He held the door open for Amy and she passed in front of him. They didn't speak at all as they walked the block to the coffee shop. It wasn't his favorite. It was a chain; impersonal, interchangeable a perfect place to end a relationship.

He grabbed a coffee for himself and green tea for Amy and they settled at a tiny round table in a quiet corner.

Once more he asked, "Why are you here?" He hadn't liked the way she put on that little scene in front of Meg. He'd seen her as possessive and manipulative and he didn't like either of those qualities.

She pushed her hair behind her ears, then looked up at him. "I saw a picture of you. I was ordering some clothing online, because I don't have time to shop, and this ad came up. I wouldn't have paid any attention except it included a picture of you in a tuxedo putting a ring on a woman's finger."

He felt a moment of pride that his online marketing was working. He'd targeted those ads to women in Amy's age group who shopped online or at vintage stores.

Even as she explained the situation to him, he felt her puzzlement in her own reaction. "The woman was wearing a wedding dress. I didn't realize it was an ad at first. I saw you and it looked like you were getting married. My first reaction was, "What have I done? What have I let go?"

She shook her head, consternation wrinkling her forehead. "I had this awful feeling, and when I stopped to read the ad and I realized that you weren't actually marrying someone without telling me, but that you were taking part in an advertising spread, well, it seemed like I needed to come back here and make things right with you." She sipped her tea. "I didn't like seeing some other woman in your wedding photo."

He was genuinely puzzled. "But, the last time we were together was awful." He didn't want to sugarcoat things. Amy had been preoccupied and busy with work, and he'd been a lot more interested in spending the time he had with his startup partners than with Amy. They'd argued, said some harsh words, and he'd cut his trip short. Maybe they hadn't said, "It's over," but he thought two months of complete silence suggested the relationship was over.

"I know. But maybe if we tried harder. I mean, it's not like you need to be in LA. I'm sure your mother and aunt could find someone else to help them out in the vintage store. I think you should come back with me."

"And do what?"

She looked at him like he was stupid. "Move in with me. I think we should try it out and see if there's any hope for us."

"When I left, I thought it was over. We maybe emailed, what, twice? Amy, it's been two months. If neither of us cared enough to email, pick up the phone, or text each other, how would it be different if we lived together?"

"I don't know." She lifted her cup off the saucer and then put it back down again without drinking. "My life's not like I thought it would be. I work all the time. I know this is what I wanted. And if I keep working as hard as I do now, I'll be a top executive within five years. But I have no social life. I don't meet people and I feel like maybe we gave up on each other too quickly."

He thought that maybe if he hadn't met Meg he might be tempted at least to think about her proposal. But he had met Meg and he understood now that what he and Amy had shared was never meant to be long term. He didn't want to hurt her, but he needed to be clear.

He reached over for her hand and clasped it loosely in his. "You are a terrific woman. You're smart, driven, sophisticated, and gorgeous. But we don't love each other. I don't want to try something out because we're afraid there's nothing better out there. We've never been the kind of people who settle. You're young, you've got everything going for you. Maybe what you need is to take a little time off work. Take a holiday, go to parties. Try dating online."

Her lips closed in a thin line and she drew her hand back. "It's her, isn't it?"

Even though he knew exactly who she was referring to, he said, "Her, who?"

Her gaze was cool and level. "Don't be an ass. That girl. The redhead. When you were talking to her in the store I recognized her from the ad. Are you in love with her?"

"Wow. I'd forgotten how a conversation with you sometimes feels like surgery without anesthetic."

She smiled a little at that.

He continued, "I know how stupid this sounds. I hardly know that woman but yeah, I think maybe I am in love with her."

She nodded. "I wish I'd never seen that picture. Then I wouldn't know what I'm missing." She glanced up. "You never looked at me that way. Two years with you and you never once looked at me the way you looked at the girl in that picture."

"How do I look at her?"

"Like she's the reason you get up in the morning."

If Meg was actually his, he'd love that description of how he was around her. But Meg wasn't his. What would he do if the woman he was crazy about didn't feel the same?

He knew one thing. He couldn't wait any longer. He needed

at least to find out whether Meg was engaged or not, and if she had any interest in him.

He said, "I'm glad you came. It's good to be clear about things."

She nodded, slowly. "I hope we can still be friends."

"I hope so, too." Though, honestly, he doubted it. Amy didn't have time to shop or date. When was she going to find time to keep up with an old flame? He felt that what they were both really saying was that there were no hard feelings. At least he hoped so.

She got up to leave, but he called her back.

"What did that girl look like in the pictures, when she looked at me?"

Her glance was scornful. "Please. I'm not here to pander to your inflated ego."

Amy was nothing if not sharp, and she noticed things. Pandering to his ego probably meant that Meg looked at him as though he were someone special, too. He felt hope spring up, and rose to follow her. "Come on, I'll walk you out."

And then, he had an important call to make.

## CHAPTER 10

*M*eg burst into the apartment she shared with June, so wildly mortified and so full of confused energy that she thought her head would explode if she didn't burn some of that energy off.

She charged towards her bedroom and heard June say, "Whoa! What's gotten into you? Somebody piss you off?"

"I can't talk about it right now." In fact, she couldn't even be inside the apartment. She needed to be outside, and she needed action. She turned to June who ran about thirty miles a week. "Where can I go jogging?"

June's eyes opened wide. "Jogging? You hate jogging."

"Which makes it the perfect activity for me right now."

"Okay." June stared at her and a crease formed in her forehead. "You want urban? Wilderness? A park?"

"Something with long trails, where I can get lost in them."

"Try Griffith Park. You can jog as long as you like, and if you still have energy you can climb up Hollywood Peak and have a great view of the city."

"Perfect." She ran to her room and changed into yoga wear, since she did not own any actual jogging clothes, and slipped into her one and only pair of sneakers. Her yoga pants were black and went to just below her knee. She threw on a sports bra and the first top she could find, which happened to be purple.

She tied her hair back, slapped a ball cap on her head, and grabbed her car keys.

Back out in the main room, she said, "Draw me a map so I can find a good jogging trail."

"Okay." June was treating her with great gentleness as though she'd recently endured a tragedy or were possibly a violent mental case. She dragged a sheet of paper off the tray of their printer and sketched out a quick map. "This is about five miles. If you still have energy when you're finished, you can just do it again."

"Thanks." She grabbed the paper.

"Water. Don't forget water."

"Right." She didn't own a fancy hydration system, what she had was a purple water bottle she took to yoga. That would have to do. She filled it with water and found her hands were not quite steady.

June watched her with growing concern. "Do you want me to come with you?"

She shook her head violently. Then realized June was being nice and said, "But thanks." All she wanted to be was alone.

"How about my iPod? Do you want to borrow it so you have music?"

"No." Her thoughts were running around her head and she felt like she just needed to sort them out. She didn't want the distraction of music.

"At least take your phone. You jogging? This worries me."

Even though she knew she was acting neurotic and jumpy, she managed to smile at that. "I'll take my phone." She grabbed her cell and realized she would have to carry all these things when she was jogging. She glanced around helplessly and June jumped up. She came back with a tiny backpack built for joggers. "Have fun. Call me if you get lost."

"I will."

She headed off but before she reached the door June admonished her one more time. "Take some money and your driver's license."

She nodded, glad somebody was thinking straight since she obviously wasn't. She collected her things and headed out once more.

Griffith Park was full of Saturday tourists and families going to the zoo, couples out having a picnic, or walking up to see the famous Hollywood sign. There were old people, young people, kids, cyclists, rollerbladers, horseback riders, and joggers. Lots of joggers. She checked the map that June had given her and took to the sketched-out path.

She hated jogging. But today, violent exercise felt like exactly what she needed. She started off imitating the pace of the jogger in front of her, but soon had to slow down when she was in danger of cardiac arrest. Once she found her pace, she let her mind roam free. The physical discomfort mirrored her mental state as she recalled again and again the moment that terrifyingly elegant woman had kissed Dylan on the mouth and announced she was his girlfriend.

It was like a recurring nightmare vision. Again and again the same scene played out in her head. The worst part was that she had no right to object to Dylan having a girlfriend: she was engaged for goodness sake. Except that she wasn't, and she had truly believed that what he felt for her might be more than friendship. That it might come close to what she felt for him.

Crazy romantic. That was the trouble. She spent too much of her life inside the covers of a novel, or within the popcorn-scented comfort of a movie theater. Fantasy was not good for a gullible romantic. Romance novels and movies should be outlawed. From now on, she decided, she was only reading dark, gritty thrillers, and maybe nonfiction. Yes, that's what she should do. She should read edifying books about philosophy and art. No! Not art, art was romantic. She looked at gorgeous paintings and always made up a story about the image. That would not do. No, she'd stick to reading about science and history.

She felt heat prickle her skin, especially the back of her neck, uncomfortable beneath the heaviness of her hair, which bumped against her neck in a very unpleasant manner. She looked at the joggers running towards her and the huge number who sped past her as though she was a broken-down car in the slow lane. They all seemed so comfortable with this horrible exercise. Some even looked happy. Runner's high. As if. She glanced at her watch. She'd been going for nine minutes. She kept running; this had to get easier.

DYLAN HAD no idea where Meg had gone but he knew he had to find her. He thought, from the little he knew about her, and the things he'd read on her roommate's blog, that she was the kind of woman who would go home and retreat to a familiar place if something was bothering her.

He'd caught a glimpse of her face when Amy had announced that she was his girlfriend, and she'd looked stricken. He couldn't stand for her to think that he was attached when he was so clearly single. Whatever was going on with her, he really needed to know the truth once and for all.

He felt a strange sense of urgency, or maybe just an eagerness to see her again, to assure her that whatever *her* story was, he was a single man. It occurred to him that even if she actually was engaged, she wasn't making much effort to see her guy, so maybe he wasn't the right man for her. Meg deserved someone who'd be there for her, who wanted to go to her movie premieres and book signings and whatever events she was involved with. If her fiancé wasn't up to the job, Dylan wanted to step in and be that man.

He pulled out his phone and realized he needed to see her, talk to her, work things out face to face. So, not many minutes after his final goodbye to Amy, he found himself knocking on Meg's door.

"Come on, come on," he said under his breath, hoping she'd be home. If she wasn't here, he had no idea where to look for her. He didn't want to call her. This was not a conversation to have on a cell.

To his relief he heard the door lock turn and then the door opened. Even as he set a foot forward to talk to Meg, he froze in place.

The woman staring back at him seemed equally shocked to see him. "What are you doing in Meg's apartment?" He asked the woman who had come into his store and tried on the wedding dress, claiming it was for a pregnant friend.

She tossed her hair. "She's my roommate. What did you do to her?"

"I didn't do anything to her."

"Well, she came here looking wild-eyed and strung out."

"I really need to talk to her."

The woman looked very much as though she didn't trust him. "She's not here."

"Do you know where she is?"

She narrowed her eyes at him like she suspected he was here to case the joint. "She's jogging."

"Jogging?" Somehow Meg had not struck him as the jogging type.

"She looked like she had some energy that needed burning off."

"I don't suppose you know where she went?"

She glared at him. "Are you the reason she came here looking crushed and broken?"

He didn't want to think of Meg hurting. He said, "Probably."

"Are you going to make things right with her?"

"Yes. I want to."

"She's at Griffith Park."

He'd never find her. "Griffith Park? There's fifty miles of trails in there."

The roommate rolled her eyes. "I drew her a map. I might as well draw you one too."

"And this is where she went?" he asked when she handed him the hand-drawn trail guide.

"It's where she said she was going."

As he was leaving he said, "Hey, how's your pregnant friend? She still in the market for a wedding dress?"

The woman didn't blush or even look embarrassed. She said, "I'm helping you find Meg. That makes us even. Don't make me snatch that map back."

He headed straight for the park. Didn't have time to go home and change into jogging clothes. He wore jeans, loafers, and a black T-shirt. When he got to the park, he followed the path the roommate had drawn for him. He began by striding along and then, frustrated, he broke into a run. He searched the faces of every runner coming towards him, but none of them was Meg. His jeans were not made to run in, his loafers certainly weren't. But he didn't want to waste one extra minute before he found Meg and told her he was single, available, and that he had feelings for her.

He jogged an uncomfortable mile, maybe two, and then he saw her coming towards him. She wasn't moving very fast. She looked overheated, her face red and streaked with sweat, her hair escaping from her ponytail in wild wisps. He thought she was the most beautiful thing he'd ever seen. "Meg!" he yelled, and ran towards her.

She didn't exactly look overjoyed to see him. Mostly, she appeared confused. She slowed to a walk. She was panting. "Dylan," she wheezed. "What are you doing here?"

"I needed to find you."

He put his hands on her shoulders. They were hot from exertion.

She looked up at him. "Why?"

Those intense brown eyes told him everything he needed to know. Words did not seem adequate to express what he wanted to say. He pulled her into his arms and kissed her.

Her lips trembled beneath his, and then she clung to him. He tasted salt from her workout. He pulled away much sooner than he wanted to, because, from the way she'd been panting, she needed the oxygen. He gazed down at her and if possible she was more flushed. "Amy's not my girlfriend."

Two young moms ran by, pushing infants in jogging strollers. He led Meg off the busy path and they found a grassy spot to sit on.

"She seemed to think she was."

He took her hand. She didn't pull away. It was old-fashioned, romantic, and he didn't care. Her hand felt right in his. A little hot and sweaty, but small and fine-boned. "She was my girl-friend in college. We tried to keep it going but she lives in San Jose. I'm here. It's true, we never officially broke up, but things petered out. I haven't seen her in two months."

"You haven't seen her for two months?"

"No. When she arrived today, I could not have been more surprised."

"Neither could I."

"I know. I'm so sorry about that."

"What made her come back now, after two months? And announce that she was your girlfriend?" she asked, still panting a little.

"She saw the pictures of us. The wedding pictures from an ad I ran online. And you know what she said?"

"What?"

"She said, that in the picture it seemed like I was crazy about you."

He felt her hands tremble. "That is a very talented photographer."

"It's true. I am crazy about you."

She made a sound sort of like a moan.

"Are you okay?"

She was flapping her hand in front of her face. "I was already breathless. Now I feel like I don't have any air."

He opened up her water bottle and handed it to her. She drank some and closed her eyes for a second.

Then he said, "I have to ask. Is there any hope for me? Is there any chance that you maybe might not get married?"

She put her hand over her eyes. He wanted to kiss her again so badly, but resisted the urge.

She said, "I'm not engaged. I never was."

After a second, she dropped her hand and looked at him, presumably to see his reaction. Then her jaw dropped. "You don't even look surprised. Did you know?"

"I didn't know for sure. But, I was hoping." He was so happy, and she was so adorable. "He's never around, you seemed to have no actual plans. You never talked about him. And, there was this thing developing between us. So, I hoped."

"You don't think I'm a crazy person?"

He laughed. "Not at all."

She leaned forward. "It was the dress. One minute, I was minding my own business, walking down Melrose on my lunch hour. And then I saw the dress and it was like it cast a spell on me. I couldn't help but walk into Joe's Past and Present and then I tried it on, and you looked at me and you asked when I was getting married, and I couldn't say I hadn't had a date in months. I just fell into fantasy."

That was a good way to put it. "We both did."

"Really?"

He stretched out his legs and leaned back on his elbows then stared up at the sky. "I'm a rational man. I write business plans and calculate profit and loss statements. I don't fall for a girl the first time I see her."

She gave him her sweet, shy smile. "You did?"

"I did."

"So, we're both single." She offered him that quirky grin that he adored.

"Are we?"

# CHAPTER 11

*W*hen she looked at him that way, nothing in the world could stop him from leaning over and pulling her closer. This time, their kiss was long, deep, and full of promise.

"I just got my breath back," she complained. She put a hand to her chest. "Now I'm breathless again." Her eyes twinkled. "But in a good way."

"I have an idea. Why don't we go back to your place and you can get cleaned up and then I'll take you out to celebrate."

Her eyes lit up. "I'd love that." And then a look of embarrassment crossed her face. "But, I'm not sure . . . My place is um, my roommate is home and she—"

"Came into Joe's and tried on your dress and pretended it was for a pregnant friend?"

"How did you know that?"

"I went by your place earlier."

"Honestly, I could have killed her when she told me she went into the store and asked about the wedding dress. I have no idea what she was doing."

"Don't worry. We're cool. How do you think I tracked you down?"

"June?"

"Is that her name?"

"Yeah. Usually she's out all the time, but she's in intense writing mode right now."

"That's okay. I'll play nice."

"Good."

"Do you want to jog back to the cars?"

"I am so done with jogging."

He laughed put a hand out and pulled her to her feet. And since he pulled a little harder than strictly necessary, she ended up chest to chest with him and he went in for another deep kiss. He felt as though he could spend the rest of his life kissing this woman and never grow tired of it.

Since they had two cars, they met back at her place. Sure enough, the roommate was on the couch working on a laptop when they got there. She glanced up and seemed relieved to see the two of them together. "Did you kiss and make up?"

He loved the way Meg blushed as she answered. "We did."

The roommate seemed genuinely happy. "Good. You two fit together."

While Meg excused herself to shower and change her clothes, he took a seat on the single chair in their small living area facing the couch. He said, "Meg mentioned that her roommate writes a dating blog. Are you by any chance Single Chick in LA?"

"How did you figure that out?"

"I stumbled across one of your posts. It was funny. About dating a bowler."

She nodded. "It was the big balls headline. Pulled a lot of traffic."

"You're a good writer."

"Thanks."

He gestured with his chin to her laptop. "Writing your latest blog post?"

"I'm going over a novel I wrote. But writing is tough. As difficult as acting."

"Most things worth doing are difficult."

"What, retail?"

"Well, running a vintage store has its challenges, but my real gig is working on a startup."

"Wow. That's cool."

"Cool, terrifying if we don't get the funding, even more terrifying if another company puts a better product out before we can get to market. But, exhilarating too."

"And then there's Meg, struggling to get her big break so she can get promoted at her agency. What is with us? Why isn't any of this easy?"

He shrugged. "I think if something's easy you're probably not trying hard enough."

"Words to live by."

They chatted for a few minutes, mostly about being single in LA, though he suspected that state was now over for him. And then Meg returned. Her hair was still wet from the shower and lay in loose, damp curls. She wore a green sundress that showed off her slender curves. And slung over her shoulder was a bag big enough that an optimist could imagine it contained at least a toothbrush and a change of clothing.

As they were leaving, June said, "Since I don't know when I'll see you again, can I email you my book and get some feedback?"

～

MEG FELT EMBARRASSED, as though June had X-ray vision and could see inside her bag where she'd slipped her makeup case, and a change of clothes in case she ended up not coming home tonight. For Meg this was a big deal, and June all but broadcasting the fact left her deeply mortified.

Then, she had the added stress of knowing that June would expect her to be an in-house editor. It brought back to her clearly the days of her last relationship, the needy writer desperate for praise, and her attempts to give helpful editorial suggestions without crushing his delicate writer's ego. It had been horrible with her boyfriend, but at least they hadn't lived together. She wasn't sure she could handle having to live with a temperamental writer who, if she praised the work, thought she was blowing smoke, and if she criticized it in even the gentlest fashion, felt that she was attacking.

However, she'd promised and it was a big deal to finish a first novel. "Congratulations on finishing the book. Sure, go ahead and send it to me." And then she and Dylan headed out the door.

He said, "You didn't seem too thrilled with the idea of reading June's manuscript."

She was so glad she was finally free to tell Dylan anything she wanted to. She told him about her last relationship and how on the one hand dating a needy author had led her to her current career and on the other hand the relationship had left her deeply distrustful of needy creative types.

"I'm no expert, but I bet June is tougher than you think. I've read her blog. She gets pretty harsh comments and actually handles them really well."

She turned to stare at him. "You've read June's blog?"

He chuckled and she felt that he was genuinely amused. "Absolutely. Single Chick in LA is my go-to place for dating advice."

"Very funny. Really, how did you stumble across her blog?"

"Wow, this is really a day for you and I to share our secrets, isn't it?"

"I like sharing secrets with you." She felt warm and intimate knowing that she could probably tell him anything and he'd understand or at least try to understand and she hoped she could do the same for him.

"I was in my favorite coffee shop over my lunch hour checking out how our ads were doing and looking to see if any fashion blogs had picked up the press release about the Evangeline gown. Somehow, her blog came up. I would have flipped past it but there was a headline about big balls that made me laugh and so I read her blog post."

"The bowler from Winnipeg."

"That very one. Then, do you know what her next post was?"

"No. Honestly, I don't have time to read her blog consistently. I hope she wasn't mean about the men in LA. You can't take it personally. She gets a little bitter sometimes."

Once more he grinned at her and she thought his smile was one of the most charming things about him. "The title of her blog post, I recall, was something like, 'How my roommate met the guy of her dreams and then pretended she was engaged.'"

Her jaw literally fell open. "She did not!"

His chuckle was truly evil. "Oh, she did."

"I am going to kill her."

"Don't. She did me such a favor. You had mentioned over dinner that your roommate wrote a blog about dating in LA. Even though there are probably hundreds of those blogs out there, something about it made me wonder. And then, when I read back over her older posts, I noticed that when she mentioned the roommate, that woman sounded like you."

"Tell me you didn't read the post about our double date."

"It was hilarious."

"If you can like me after that, anything is possible."

"Oh, liking you is the least I can do."

They drove through the evening and found a small bistro with an outdoor patio. Now that her secret was out and they were free to be honest about their feelings, they couldn't seem to stop talking. About everything from her hopes and fears about her future at the agency to his about his startup. After dinner, he said, "I have to take you to my favorite place for gelato."

"You have a favorite gelato place?" It seemed completely adorable. Then, she was so far gone that everything he did seemed completely adorable.

"I do. It's run by Italians and the chocolate espresso is amazing."

The gelato place was in a fairly quiet neighborhood and while he did order his espresso chocolate, she went for something slightly less caffeinated and chose pistachio mint. Naturally they had to try each other's gelato, and then they had to kiss so she tasted chocolate coffee mint pistachio all at once and decided it was a new flavor sensation that ought to be on the recipe board.

Afterwards, they walked out hand-in-hand. He seemed to have a destination in mind so she was happy to follow along. He paused. He had a disturbing glint in his eyes. "Do you know what's in that building on the third floor?"

This was clearly a residential building and she didn't think they were visiting a friend for coffee. "Your apartment?"

He nodded. "Would you like to come up?"

She appreciated that he didn't make any pretense of offering her coffee or brandy or something. He was clearly asking her if she felt comfortable spending time alone with him. She paused for a second and realized that from the moment she'd walked up to that dress and bumped her nose on the window of Joe's Past and Present, this moment had been inevitable. She said, "Yes. I would love to see your apartment."

He led her into the building, up the elevator and to his suite. Every step of the way she felt herself moving closer to the inevitable. He opened the door of his apartment and held it so that she could walk in ahead of him. He put on a light and she saw that the furniture was a little on the shabby side but nice, good-quality pieces. Probably from auctions or things that came through the vintage store. He wasn't particularly tidy nor was he very messy; his place looked lived in. His copy of *Pride and Prejudice* lay on the coffee table beside the couch and she could tell that this was his favorite reading spot.

He turned her and kissed her softly. "I don't want to rush this, our first time together. Let's make it memorable."

She felt nervous and jumpy and yet wildly excited. A few hours ago, she'd been pounding down a jogging trail believing any hope of her and Dylan being together was over. Now it seemed they were a couple. She felt that her body and mind needed a chance to keep up to the changing circumstances of her life. "I agree."

He kissed her mouth and then her cheeks, tiny butterfly wings of kisses. "I want to know everything about you."

How seductive to have someone want to know everything. And how terrifying. She simply wasn't that interesting a person.

She felt as though every molecule in her body was straining towards him.

Then he turned her so her back was to him. He kissed the back of her neck. His voice was low as he said, "I am so glad you wore a dress with buttons down the back. I've been fantasizing all night about the first time I saw you. The first time you came into the store and you tried on the wedding dress."

As he spoke he slowly and carefully released the first button and then leaned forward and pressed his lips to the skin he'd revealed. Shivers of desire chased up and down her spine. She had not slipped into the dress intentionally but she had to wonder if, on some subconscious level, she had reimagined their first meeting, too.

"Do you have any idea how much I wanted you that day?" He slipped another button free and once more pressed his lips to the skin of her upper back. She remembered so well that first day even as he'd been both professional and impersonal, it was impossible for him to unbutton the dress without his fingers touching her. Oh, she would never forget the feel of his fingers brushing her skin but that was nothing compared to the feel of his lips tracing the same path now, each of them openly accepting their desire.

With each button slipped out of its buttonhole he grew closer to his goal. But he was not a man in a hurry. She felt that he was savoring every moment, drawing out this slow, tortuous seduction. Her cotton dress might as well have been a silk and satin wedding gown for all the care he took with each button. She felt the ever-so-slight coolness as more skin was revealed. The moist pressure as his lips progressed slowly down her spine, the waft of his soft breath.

Never had she imagined her back as one of her most eroge-nous zones but with this careful seduction she felt every inch of her to be hot, hot to the point of melting under his lips and hands. He reached the end of the buttons at last and ran the pads of his fingers all the way down to the bottom of the V where her dress gaped. She wore no bra, another reason she'd chosen this dress. "I think you have the sexiest back I've ever seen," he said, his voice growing husky. He slipped the straps over her shoulders and the cotton slid slowly down her body. Naturally, she was wearing her best panties. They were pale blue silk with lace panels, an indulgence she had not been able to resist.

He turned her slowly to face him, and she felt that she was all but naked while he remained fully clothed. Her skin was ultrasensitive. He kissed her and then drew back, gazing down at her near-naked body. "You're even more beautiful than I imagined," he said.

As much as she wanted to drag his clothes off, and fast, she also took her time. There could only ever be one first time for them and she wanted this to be special. She untucked his shirt from his jeans and lifted the hem, slowly, revealing his torso inch by inch in the same way he had bared her back, only going backwards so she first revealed his lower abs, tight and ridged with muscle. She bent and put her lips there. And then a little higher. His skin was hot and while she worked her way slowly up his belly, his hands were busy in her hair, caressing her shoulders, her back, every bit of her that he could reach.

At the end he helped her pull his shirt up and over his head and then tossed it to the floor. He wasn't particularly big or bulky, but had defined muscles and a strength to him that she liked. When he pulled her in for another deep kiss her breasts rubbed against his chest, sending delicious shivers through her. She felt his excitement press against her and it fired hers. It seemed as though they had run out of patience, for even as she reached for the button of his jeans, he was there before her unbuttoning, zipping, yanking, hopping on one foot to free himself of the last of his clothing and then finally standing before her naked.

"Come on," he said, grabbing her hand and leading her into the bedroom. She paused at the door. She'd done nothing about birth control and, much as she hated to throw cold water on the proceedings, she had to ask before she lost her head. "Condoms?"

"Taken care of," he said.

"Good." She sighed in relief. And followed him. She had the vaguest impression of a large bed, gray duvet cover, more of that solid, dark furniture. A bookcase. He laid her down on his bed and began to kiss his way down her body. He slid her panties off, and dropped them over the side of the bed, then pulled the covers over them so she felt warm, and protected, and so very excited.

She felt tension in every line of his body. And she understood that this moment mattered, that she mattered.

He was so beautiful to her and as he looked into her eyes, she felt that she was beautiful to him too. They toyed with each other, learning each other's bodies, touching, caressing, stretching out the anticipation until neither of them could wait any longer. He reached into his bedside drawer and grabbed a condom, then sheathed himself swiftly and efficiently.

She parted her legs for him and he entered her slowly, his gaze intent on hers and she knew that whatever happened, this moment would be etched in her mind forever as one of the most perfect moments of her life. And then they began to move and she could no longer hold onto one coherent thought.

Joined. The word lodged in her mind as she felt him inside the very deepest part of her. He clasped her hands in his and she wrapped her legs around him. Joined, that's how she felt and even once their lovemaking was over she knew that in some way she would always be joined to him.

# CHAPTER 12

*W*hen she woke up the next morning the first thing she saw was her brand-new lover beside her in bed. He was asleep and had one arm flung over her, his face already shadowed with morning stubble. She thought she could get used to waking up to Dylan. Perhaps her scrutiny woke him, for his eyes opened sleepily. And as they settled on her face, green with darker flecks that fascinated her, he smiled, a slow, sexy smile. "Good morning. Did you get any sleep?"

She grinned, and stretched, memories of that long, delicious night rippling through her. "Not much."

She felt different. As though the world was colored a little brighter and her emotions were a little higher, her senses sharper. Even though they'd barely slept, she bounced out of bed full of energy. He put on coffee while she showered and they made breakfast together. Eggs and toast and fresh fruit.

She hadn't said the words last night but she had felt them in every cell of her body. She loved this man. She loved his sexy green eyes and morning stubble, his intelligence and his humor.

They talked for a long time over coffee, and then he said, "I'm heading into the store this afternoon for a couple of hours.

But otherwise I'm free. Maybe we could go to the beach later. Or grab a movie or anything you like."

She loved that he was planning his day with her in it. Like a good boyfriend. Even as the word boyfriend skittered through her mind, she shied away from it. She did not want to get ahead of herself. She needed to take this one day at a time and be happy for every moment they had together. Besides, she had a pile of work to do at home. She said, "I've got a pile of manuscripts I need to get through, but I can take my work to the beach."

"Cool." He put away the dishes that he'd washed and she'd dried. "I'll drop you back home and then call you later."

"I'd be devastated if you didn't. I wish they'd pick the new agent so I could stop stressing."

He glanced at her with sympathy. "Still haven't found the next Pride and Prejudice?"

"Not even a Catch-22."

"Tell you what, the beach isn't going anywhere. How about you bring your work over and I'll cook you dinner tonight?"

She blinked. Instead of being demanding of her time, he wanted to help her. Her love pretty much doubled in that second. "Why am I not surprised that you cook?"

"I have no patience with men who can't do domestic chores. Growing up with a single mom I learned to cook, clean and do laundry. I'm also pretty handy with a hammer."

"Joe did a good job with you."

He grinned at her. "Thanks. I'll tell her you think so."

He dropped her off back at her place, kissed her thoroughly, and then went on to work.

She tried to focus, she really did. But she'd be reading a manuscript and suddenly become aware that she had no idea what the story was about. Her mind was wandering like a girl with her first crush. She wondered, what was Dylan doing? Was he thinking about her?

She grew so irritated that she forced herself to put Dylan, and the events of last night, out of her mind and concentrate only on her reading. This lasted approximately five minutes until her cell phone rang and she saw that it was Dylan calling. She said, "Hi," and felt all warm and sexy that he'd called her already.

She very much hoped that he was as distracted as she was.

He kept his voice low. "I thought I'd tell you that my aunt is working today. This might be a great opportunity to practice your impersonation of a shark."

She squealed with delight. "Really? What kind of a mood would you say she's in?"

"A good mood."

"Great. Are you going to tell her that I'm coming?"

"Negative. I don't want her thinking I tried to manipulate her. That works against you."

"Got it. I'll just wander in looking for . . . I'll think of something I need."

"Got to go. Can't wait to see you."

Meg had managed to get through the better part of three manuscripts. Nothing called to her. Two were very competently written, interesting enough in their own way, but not outstanding enough that she felt the agency could do anything with them. She had two more paper manuscripts and one more computer file to go through. June had also emailed her a manuscript. She knew she would need to look at it in the next couple of days but today, when she was so happy, she did not want to have to try and think up diplomatic ways to tell her roommate that her first novel sucked.

It wasn't uncommon, most first novels sucked, but she didn't have to live with all the other first-time novelists whose manuscripts she turned down.

Fortunately, June had been out all day. She had not had to

deal with one needy author in her space, only manuscripts of half a dozen needy authors that she would likely never meet.

She dressed with care to go back to Joe's Past and Present, putting on a wrap dress that was easy to slip off since she would be trying on clothes. She thought that if she was going to stop by Joe's she had better do some shopping to disguise her intention. Though, of course, Dylan's aunt was a very intelligent woman and would no doubt see right through her ruse.

She took extra care with her makeup and hair, and that was not for Dylan's aunt's benefit but for Dylan himself. The thought of seeing him again, even though they'd only seen each other a few hours ago, filled her with excitement. She really had it bad.

When she strolled fake-casually into Joe's the store was surprisingly busy. Dylan handled the cash desk while his aunt helped customers. She took her time browsing, while surreptitiously keeping an eye on Dylan's aunt. She wore yet another vintage gown today. She looked elegant, retro, and kind of funky. Meg loved her style.

Dylan had not seen her yet, he was too busy ringing up purchases and bagging items. He glanced up from the last customer with a cheerful, "Thanks for waiting. Come back soon."

Then he caught sight of her. Since she was already watching him she had the pleasure of seeing how glad he was to see her. His face lit up and he gave her a big smile and then beckoned her over. She came behind the counter; there were half a dozen people in the lineup. In front of all of them he reached over and gave her a quick kiss. "Can you help me back here for a few minutes?"

She felt the thrill of being included as though she were part of his life, part of Joe's. Since the Evangeline wedding gown was safely hanging in the display window she had no fears about helping move merchandise. "No problem."

And so, as he rang up the purchases she stood beside him doing her best to fold every item neatly and place it in the bags that were stacked beneath the counter. When the rush ended, Dylan's aunt came up to them. Her eyebrows rose when she saw Meg behind the cash desk and Dylan quickly said, "It was crazy back here. I had a lineup eight people deep so Meg jumped in to help bag purchases."

"That was nice of you, Meg. It's good to see you again."

"Great to see you again too. I love your outfit."

Janet Delaney looked down at herself in peach silk and shrugged. "It's a little over the top for daytime wear, but I thought it might help move merchandise. Besides, there's just something about the flapper era that calls to my heart."

"Have you ever felt you were born, not into the wrong time exactly, but that a certain era of clothing was made for you?"

Dylan's aunt stared at her as though she were telepathic. "Yes. Exactly. It's not that I believe in reincarnation, but I've always been drawn to this era, to these clothes and Deco architecture and jewelry. Even the books of that time."

Meg nodded, enthusiastically. "*A Movable Feast, The Great Gatsby*, I know."

"Is that your era, too?"

She shook her head. "I think, for me, it would be Regency England. The muslin dresses and bonnets, I would not have wanted to live in that time, though. I'm too attached to indoor plumbing, antibiotics, and my computer."

"I wish we had something for you in the store, but of course, anything surviving from that time would be almost impossible to find apart from in museums and private collections."

She sighed. "The one thing I most want in this store is that wedding gown hanging in the window," she admitted.

Janet shook her head in amazement. "Honestly, I think if we had fifty of those dresses we could sell them all. I've never seen anything like it. I've had three women in today practically demanding to buy it. I thought one was actually going to throw a fit when I told her she could not have it. She said it was hers."

"I know how she feels," Meg admitted. "There is something about that gown that brings out the romantic in all of us. I'm not even engaged, yet I feel like that dress was meant for me."

Dylan glanced up. "Oh, it was."

Janet glanced shrewdly between the two of them and she had a feeling that she could see the brand-new intimacy between them. She was determined not to blush.

A couple of young men walked in and Dylan said, "I'll go help those guys."

As he left, she felt that he was giving her a chance to talk to Janet privately. Since she had no idea how long it would be until the next horde of shoppers entered the vintage store, she grabbed her chance with both hands. She said, "Have you thought anymore about what I said, last time we met? I would love to take you for lunch and talk about your experiences."

Janet Delaney had about three decades of experience on her and had travelled around the world. She was nothing if not sophisticated. She smiled gently and said, "I would love to have lunch with you and talk about my travel experiences and my writing. I think you're a very interesting young woman and I suspect that we have a lot in common. However, I have to be honest with you, after our last conversation I called my agent and asked how they would feel about me working on a film project with another agency." She shook her head. "They have a film agent based in LA and they have sent all my books for consideration. I've been with that agency for more than twenty years. I have to be loyal. They've been very good to me. I'm sorry."

Meg tried to hide the crushing sense of disappointment she felt. It seemed like a gift from fate when she had bumped into Dylan's aunt and discovered that the woman was a famous travel writer. However, she hid her disappointment as best she could. "I understand. And I would still love to have lunch with you. As I said before, I am a huge fan of your work."

She got a genuine smile in return. "Thank you."

Meg asked, "How long do you think you can keep that dress, the Evangeline gown, before you have to sell it?"

"Well, that's really up to Joe and me. And Dylan of course, since he does all our marketing. It's definitely brought in a lot of business but we can't keep it forever."

"I know. I only wish I had the money to buy it now."

Janet glanced at her in surprise. "You said you aren't engaged."

This time she did blush, and couldn't help her gaze flicking to Dylan and back again. "I know. But I feel like once you have a great dress, then when the guy comes along you're ready."

Janet laughed. And her gaze followed Meg's. "So that's the way it is. Well, I don't know you very well but I like you a hell of a lot more than that stick insect he was dating before you."

Meg giggled and then said, one woman to another, "She was in here yesterday. She did seem kind of terrifying."

"Yes. I heard about that. And the little scene she put on for your benefit."

"Why would she do something like that? Dylan said he hadn't even seen her for two months."

"I would be willing to bet that she somehow heard about you and like many a woman before, never loved a man so much as when she was in danger of losing him."

"He is pretty special."

"Dylan? Oh, he is that. I like you two together. The energy I feel between you."

Okay so she didn't have a new client as a stepping stone to a job promotion, but maybe it was more important that someone Dylan liked and respected welcomed Meg as a new addition into his life.

When he came back he said, "I've got some good news I can't wait to tell you about later."

"Well, I can't wait to hear it."

"We'll be closing the store in an hour, why don't I swing by your place and pick you up?"

His aunt who was in easy earshot turned around. "Dylan, sweetheart. I'll close up tonight. There's only an hour left and I don't think we'll see another rush like we did. If we do, they'll just have to be patient."

"Are you sure?"

"Absolutely. It's a beautiful day. You should get out and enjoy it."

"Okay. Thanks."

When they headed out he said, "Let's go back to Griffith Park and take a walk."

She wrinkled her nose. "Griffith Park? Really? It has very bad memories for me."

He gave her quizzical look, "It has pretty good memories for me."

"Okay, I can get past the jogging experience and then the rest was definitely pretty good."

He glanced down at her feet. "Can you walk in those shoes?"

They were flat leather sandals and next to her sneakers her most comfortable footwear. "I can."

"Perfect." They took his car to Griffith Park and chose a different path, hiking up near the observatory so they looked out over the city. He took her hand and said, "You know what I did this morning?"

She didn't think he was referring to their early morning lovemaking session, so she said, "What?"

"I moved a stack of men's plaid shirts into the ladies lingerie area."

She giggled. "You did?"

"Oh yeah." He was openly grinning now. "And then some

poor woman had to call my name three times before I realized she needed help. My concentration was completely shot." He leaned closer and brushed a stray curl off her cheek, "I kept thinking about you, and last night." He closed the distance between them and kissed her.

When they finally pulled away, she said, "I tried to work on manuscripts and, honestly, I can't remember what a single one of them was about. I would be reading and ten pages would have gone by and well, I was thinking of the same things you were."

"Glad I'm not the only one."

"You aren't."

He kissed her again and then, when their walk veered towards X-rated she said, "What's the good news you wanted to tell me about?"

"Oh, right. My partners called me earlier. Our software is ready for beta testing."

She was no computer expert but that sounded very good. "Wow, that's great!"

"Three years of hard work have gone into this. We could be on the market within six months." He sounded really excited. "This could be my big break."

"I'm so excited for you and your colleagues."

"I'm probably going to have to stop working at Joe's for a bit and put all my efforts into the startup. Luckily Aunt Janet is around, so she can take over for me."

"That's good."

He nudged her. "Which will give you more opportunities to stalk her."

She shook her head. It was a good thing one of them had good news on the career front. She said, "She was very honest with me. She talked to her agent in New York and they claim they already have some agents looking at her stuff for a possible film. She's not going to piss off her main agent, she's too loyal."

He nodded, looking sympathetic. "I'm sorry."

She shrugged. "I'm no worse off than I was a few days ago before I had ever met your aunt. I just need to keep looking. The right project is out there, I just have to find it." And soon. She had heard that the senior agents were going to make a decision within the next couple of weeks. While she knew her work was excellent and she was reliable and tremendously good at getting things done, and their clients liked her, it wasn't enough. She had to bring in new clients and projects if she wanted to be an agent and not spend her life as an assistant.

As though he could read her mind he rubbed a hand down her back. "Don't worry. Things will work out."

"I hope you're right."

At least one area of her life seemed to be going amazingly well.

# CHAPTER 13

*T*hey sat for a while telling their stories and catching each other up on their lives to date. Everything about him was fascinating to her and she realized that, as relatively uninteresting as her life had been, he found her fascinating, too.

She suspected that was the thing about love. It made an ordinary person seem extraordinary. Not that there was anything ordinary about Dylan. And she didn't think that was her emotions clouding her judgment. He was a man who chose to work on a startup instead of taking a steady job with a good paycheck. He was a man who didn't feel that his masculinity was threatened by working in a vintage store. She felt that he knew who he was and was very comfortable in his own skin. She also believed that Dylan was a man who was destined for success. Their software would genuinely help people to stay safer on the Internet. She liked that he was working on something important.

After they had shared confidences in the late afternoon sunshine, they decided to head back to his place where he'd promised to cook her dinner. She could imagine nights and nights of dinners at home. It was too easy to see a future stretch, too much as though she were writing her own happily-ever-after. And yet, she felt that, for her, meeting Dylan had been a defining moment in her life. Whatever happened, there would be a before Dylan and an after Dylan. She only hoped that he'd continue to star in the after-meeting-Dylan portion of her story.

They bought fresh fish, the makings of a salad, crusty bread and a bottle of wine, and then they headed back to his place. She made the salad while he prepared fish and warmed the bread. He poured the wine and even lit candles so that when they sat down to eat at his small table it was as romantic as the fanciest French restaurant.

He raised his glass. "I would like to propose a toast."

She raised her glass and watched the candlelight wink against her white wine. He said, "To the wedding-gown designer Evangeline for bringing us together."

Such a delightful toast and so absolutely perfect that she echoed, "To Evangeline."

Then she bit into her fish, perfectly cooked and said, "Mmm. You really can cook." She liked that they were eating at home, without the intrusion of waiters and the fuss of ordering. She liked that he'd cooked for her.

When they were done with dinner he said, "Do you want to go get some gelato for dessert?"

She shook her head. "You know what I want for dessert?"

There was a disturbing gleam in his eyes as though he knew exactly what she was about to say. She said, "I want you."

They never made it to the bedroom. She discovered that the couch in the living room was exactly as comfortable as it looked.

Monday she had to be at work early so she left Dylan's place and headed back to hers. In the early morning she crept in, showered, changed, and headed to work. Already she was wondering if she should leave a few essentials at Dylan's place even though she knew it was way too soon to be commandeering cupboard or drawer space. She wondered how long a woman had to wait before being granted shelf space in a man's house. Was there some unspoken rule? Somehow, she felt that the regular rules were never going to apply with her and Dylan. Their relationship seemed to be headed on a path all its own.

Even though she had a fat load of nothing to offer the senior agents, she couldn't help the good mood that carried her into work. Even when Anthony Rowen came into her cubicle with his normal Monday-morning serious expression and warned her that the future of the company depended on her, and even when she overheard that one of the other assistants—a young sci-fi and fantasy geek—had signed a promising new client with a trilogy that was meant to rival *Game of Thrones*, she refused to panic.

Her time would come. Normally, she'd never be this complacent. Great sex did wonders for putting her career angst into perspective.

She was working hard, and she was doubling her efforts to figure out a strategy for finding the project or client that would boost her career. She'd joined a writer's group and an Indie film club, hoping to scoop the next great talent and she was combing through the endless slush pile hoping for treasure.

As busy as she and Dylan both were, they spent every night together. She'd never known she could be this happy. It was almost frightening, as though something menacing must be waiting around the corner to smash her bliss.

It happened on Friday.

Her day began as usual, and after a busy morning she thought maybe Dylan would like a lunch break. She called and he answered right away, but his voice sounded strained. She wished she'd swallowed her impulse to call. She knew he was working crazy hours. "Did I catch you at a bad time?"

There was a pause and then he said, "No. Not really."

"I was wondering if you wanted to get away for lunch?"

There was another pause. He said, "I think maybe you should come by the store."

"Joe's? I thought you were working at home today."

"I was. But we have a situation."

For some reason her heart began hammering in her chest. She pictured break-ins, explosions or fires. For a second she pictured her dress up in flames and she nearly moaned. Then she remembered that people were more important than clothing and asked, "Is everybody okay?"

"Yes. Everyone's fine. Come over and I'll explain."

She didn't even close her current computer file, she just grabbed her bag and ran. Something about Dylan's voice had filled her with an impending sense of doom.

It was too close to take the car so she pretty much jogged the few blocks to Joe's Past and Present. Her sense of unease grew when she saw that the window display had changed. No longer did the Evangeline wedding gown hold pride of place in center stage with the dwindling supply of bridesmaid dresses surrounding it. Instead, there was a kind of retro fifties beach scene, with a picnic basket and full-skirted cotton dresses. She pushed through the door and the bells sounded far too cheerful.

Dylan, Joe and Janet were standing in a circle looking concerned. Fortunately, there was no one else in the store. She approached them and asked, "What's going on?"

She was happy to note that there was no fire damage, the roof hadn't fallen in, and clearly the three people most involved in the shop were all perfectly healthy and safe. But all three looked at her and she saw concern and sadness in all of their faces.

Joe finally said, "Dylan, you'd better tell her."

He walked forward and took her hand. "It's the Evangeline gown."

"Oh, no." Somehow she'd known it was the gown. She felt as though lead weights had taken up residence in her belly. "What about it?"

He said, "It's been stolen."

Her eyes opened wide. "What?"

Janet stepped forward. "I'm so sorry, it was my fault."

Dylan shook his head. "No. It was my fault. I never should have taken so much time off this week and left you alone in the store yesterday afternoon."

Janet took up the tale. "It got busy yesterday afternoon. Joe was taking a day off and I was on my own. It was no big deal, I could handle it. But, of course, I couldn't keep an eagle eye on every single customer. A woman who had been in earlier insisted on trying on the Evangeline wedding gown. I took it off the mannequin and placed it in the changing room and then half-a-dozen people suddenly came in. Two women were searching for costumes for a play." She looked at Meg in apology. "It was *Private Lives*, set in the roaring twenties. You know those twenties clothes, they're my weakness. So, maybe I gave those two a little extra attention. Anyway, I closed up for the night and I didn't even notice the dress was gone. It was Joe who noticed."

Meg turned to Joe, anxiety pulling at her, mutely asking for an explanation.

"When I got to the store this morning, the mannequin in the window was naked. I assumed the dress somehow got left in the fitting room, but the gown was gone."

"Do you remember what the woman looked like?" she asked Janet.

"No. Not really. I served a lot of customers yesterday. I can't remember each one."

"Did she say anything? Did she give any indication as to when she was getting married or why she wanted the dress?"

"No. But she left a note in the change room. It said, 'I'm taking back the dress. It's mine.'"

This was the strangest theft Meg had ever heard of. "What kind of thief leaves a note?"

"I know." Janet looked as heartbroken as she felt. She'd pretty much let slip how much that dress meant. "None of us can figure it out. The thief only took one thing."

She mulled over the strange note. "Could it be the woman who brought the dress here in the first place?"

"That's what Dylan thinks," Joe said.

"But then why wouldn't she just ask for it back? Why go to all the trouble of stealing it? She probably waited until you and Dylan weren't in the store, since you both knew what she looked like."

Joe shook her head. "Everyone who puts something on consignment signs a contract. We hold on to the merchandise for at least thirty days. That's the agreement. And, she had to know, that if she asked for it back I would have refused. We've invested advertising money into the dress and that has been bringing in a lot of customers. Plus," her face softened, "that dress was yours."

"And now it's gone," she wailed. She felt the way she had the time her family got a brand-new puppy and it ran away from home. She'd been so in love with that dog. She remembered the aching sense of loss and tragedy that had engulfed her. Luckily, they recovered Trixie within two days and the dog had been a valued member of their family until she died fifteen years later.

The wedding gown had to be like Trixie. They had to get it back.

She read enough thrillers and mysteries and crime dramas in her job that she was pretty savvy about investigating. She said,

"What we need is the original contract of the woman who brought in the dress."

"Right, she's right," Dylan agreed.

Joe looked from one to the other. "What are you planning to do?"

He moved to stand beside Meg. He put an arm around her shoulders. "We're going after that dress."

CHAPTER 14

*D*ylan pushed some keys on the computer. "Here it is. Her name is Tasmine Ford. She lives in Venice Beach."

"Okay. Good."

He printed the contact information off the computer and then looked at her with some concern. "What exactly is our plan?"

Even if she knew on some level that she wasn't being entirely rational, Meg had to get that dress back. She said, "Who knows why she took it back. Maybe she's selling it privately. I need to talk to her. I need to tell her that the dress is mine."

She saw the other three exchange glances but she chose to ignore them. She'd worry about looking crazy later: for now, she had a wedding gown to trace.

Joe had never mentioned Meg's supposed engagement and seemed quite happy to have her dating her son, so Meg assumed Dylan had told her that Meg had been single all along. She seemed to have taken the news okay, but Meg didn't want to do too many more irrational things. She wanted Joe to believe she was good for Dylan, not some flake who went crazy for a dress she had no business buying.

She began to pace. "We could drive to her place. That gives us the element of surprise."

He nodded. "Or, we could phone her. Which has the element of being more reasonable and not wasting our time if she gave it away to somebody else."

"No. If she was going to be reasonable she would have talked to Joe, or Janet, or you about taking the dress back. She wouldn't have stolen it."

"You're right. This wasn't the action of a reasonable person." Like chasing after it was.

He glanced at his phone to check the time. "I need to finish up what I'm working on. She's probably at work now, anyway. What if I pick you up after work?"

"Whatever you want."

She kissed him because even though she was acting crazy he was completely on her side. She thought that a man who would stand by her no matter what was a good man to have in her life.

They met back after work. She'd sketched out a sort of strategy of what she would say when she saw this Tasmine Ford.

Dylan drove, and as they headed toward Venice Beach she asked, "Did you see the woman who brought in the dress?"

"I did."

"What was she like?"

He took a moment to answer and she imagined he was pulling up a mental file. "She was blonde, nice-looking, cheer-leader type. She told Joe that she was in sales and seemed very interested in how the dress would be marketed. She was also the one who brought in all those bridesmaid dresses." He glanced over at her. "There were like twelve of them. All in her size. She'd been a bridesmaid at more than a dozen weddings."

"I can't even imagine."

"I know."

"And she didn't steal any of those dresses back?"

"No."

"What do you think that says about a person? You know the old saying, always a bridesmaid never a bride."

"I don't know. She really likes weddings? Has a lot of friends?"

She felt that there was a mystery here and a vital clue was missing. They found the address Tasmine Ford had given and arrived at a nicely kept apartment building. They got out of the car together, like a pair of cops, and approached the intercom pad. She said, "I hope she's home."

"Have you thought about what you're going to say?"

"I've practiced fifty times."

They rang the apartment buzzer but there was no answer.

"She could be out."

"She could be meeting someone who answered her online ad and be selling the dress right at this moment. She probably saw the advertising you were doing and realized she could get the full five grand."

"We can't think that way. We have to be positive."

She let out a huge sigh. "Okay, should we call her?"

He pulled out the printout with Tasmine's contact info. "She gave two numbers, a cell and her work number."

They tried her cell first and it went to voicemail. All she learned was that Tasmine Ford had a very nice speaking voice. She could imagine that voice in sales—she sounded enthusiastic and really sorry to have missed Meg's call. Meg was really sorry too.

She checked the time; it was six o'clock. "Any chance she might still be at work?"

He shrugged. "We can try."

She dialed the work number and a jovial sounding man picked up. "Crosswells' Quality Furnishings," he said. Like Tasmine, he exuded enthusiasm.

"Hello. I'm looking for Tasmine Ford."

"You won't find her here."

If she pretended she was a customer, the man on the other end of the phone would try to solve her issue. She put on her friendliest tone. "It's really important that I find her. I'm an old friend from school. "

He chuckled. "You might have to wait until tomorrow to see her at Judge and Mrs. Bailey's place"

"Right," she said. "Was that in Malibu?"

"No, honey. Manhattan Beach."

"Of course. Thank you."

"Probably see you there."

*Probably see you there?* She had no idea what that was about but after thanking the man and hanging up, she said, "She's going to be at some judge's house tomorrow."

"Should we call?"

She shook her head. "She works for a furniture place. She's probably delivering furniture or something. If we catch her at work in front of her customers she'll be a lot easier to deal with."

"You're wasted as an agent. You should be a cop. The bad cop."

She and Dylan stopped for pizza on the way back to his place. When she got there, June texted her. *Did you read the manuscript yet?*

She felt guilt mixed with irritation. Why couldn't she find a roommate who wanted to be a painter or a musician or something she knew absolutely nothing about?

She texted back, *I'll read it this weekend. Have comments by Sunday night.*

Saturday, they drove to Manhattan Beach, she and Dylan. She had dressed with care, thinking that if Tasmine was delivering furniture to a judge's house, well, it sounded like it might be a formal sort of place. Besides, she felt that a businesslike transaction needed a businesslike appearance. So, she put on one of her favorite summer dresses. It was blue and she wore it with a cream-colored linen jacket. Dylan was a little more casual in navy slacks and an open-necked shirt.

Finding the address had been as easy as a Google search.

As they drove to Manhattan Beach they strategized. "We won't accuse her of anything," Dylan said.

"Of course not. We want to keep her speaking to us. This is purely a negotiation."

"She was going to get forty percent of five grand. Maybe she realized how much action that dress was getting. Maybe she wants a bigger cut."

He looked over at Meg and then took her hand. "Let's just offer the full five thousand."

She smiled at him. "I like the way you said we."

He shook his head. "I know it sounds crazy, but I think of us as we. It's too soon, we both know it's too soon, but I want you to have that dress. I think, unless things really change in the next few months, you'll be wearing the dress and I'll be standing at the other end of the aisle watching you walk towards me."

She felt emotion catching her throat. "Dylan. Are you proposing?"

He gave a nervous laugh and loosened a tie he wasn't wearing. "It kind of came out that way, didn't it?"

"You don't sound too sure."

"I don't think I've ever been surer of anything but I want to do this right. We should definitely spend more time getting to know each other but, I think you can consider yourself proposed to."

She'd always been a cautious woman. But sometimes, like now, she absolutely knew. She said, "Can I consider myself engaged?"

"Are you saying yes?"

She threw her head back against the head rest. "This is the most unromantic marriage proposal in history."

"I know. It sucks. I don't even have a ring."

"Well, let's call ourselves pre-engaged and in a few months we'll reassess the situation."

"That sounds very businesslike of you. I accept."

She felt very close to being the happiest woman on earth, and suspected that if, on the return journey, her wedding dress came with them that she would, in fact, be the happiest person in the world.

When they arrived at Judge Bailey's house, at two in the afternoon she felt a sudden qualm of nerves. "What if she's not here?"

He held her hand reassuringly. "Don't worry. We've got this."

She checked her hair, added another swipe of lipstick and then decided she was combat ready. They walked up to the door hand-in-hand and Dylan rang the bell.

The door was answered by a young woman wearing a maid's uniform. He said, "We're looking for Tasmine Ford."

The woman broke into a smile. "Come, right this way," she said in a strong Eastern European accent. Instead of inviting them into the house she stepped out. "It was such a beautiful day, they wanted to do it outside."

She and Dylan exchanged a glance. Wanted to do what outside? The young woman said, "How do you know Tasmine?"

"We went to school together," Meg said, repeating the same story she'd come up with the day before.

"She seems very nice."

Meg had no idea whether that was true or not since she'd never actually met the woman but she said, "Yes, she is." And hoped very much that it was true.

They followed the maid down a path that rounded the Spanish-style mansion and as they came around to the back garden her feet stopped moving and she said, "Oh."

Ahead of them was a beautiful garden and in the middle of the garden stood a white, wooden gazebo. A minister stood there and with him was a gorgeous young man who looked a little like Ryan Gosling. He was wearing a tuxedo. Rows of chairs faced the gazebo and these chairs were filled with an assortment of people all dressed in their best clothes. A harp played softly. "I'll put you on the bride's side," the maid said.

Meg was about to say that there had been a terrible mistake, when at some mysterious signal, the harp stopped playing and the unmistakable strains of 'Here Comes the Bride' sprang from an orchestra hidden from their view. "Quickly, quickly," the maid said and ushered them forward.

Meg was so stunned that she sat in the chair the woman assigned her and then the maid scurried back around and inside the house. Dylan leaned in and said softly, "I guess now we know why she wanted the dress."

Meg almost couldn't look. She didn't want to see her dress being worn by another bride. It seemed all wrong.

A smiling young woman with black hair and a nose ring twinkling in the sun began walking up the grass aisle. She wore a bright-green dress and carried a bouquet made of natural-looking roses that Meg thought might have come from this garden. They had an untamed look very different from a florist's bouquet. There was only one bridesmaid and then the bride herself appeared.

"That's her," Dylan whispered. "That's Tasmine Ford."

That might be Tasmine Ford, but at the first glimpse Meg could see that the bride was not wearing the Evangeline wedding gown.

She sat there, stunned and confused. She couldn't help but notice how truly happy the bride looked. She glanced up at the groom and Meg saw such love on his face that, even though she didn't know these people, she felt her eyes mist with emotion.

The wedding ceremony was simple but beautiful. The couple

were both tall and good-looking, but most of all they seemed happy and relaxed with each other. When they said their vows, Dylan slipped his hand into hers and squeezed. She squeezed back. She supposed it was perfect that on the day he had accidentally proposed to her they should find themselves accidentally attending a wedding.

When the minister said, "You may kiss the bride," she sighed.

The way the groom looked as he turned to his new bride was magical. When they kissed she knew how they felt. It was the way she felt when Dylan kissed her.

The pair walked back down the aisle, husband-and-wife, and Meg stood with the rest of the wedding guests and clapped as enthusiastically as any of them. Then an older man rose from the front row where the family sat and said, "Please join us in the garden room for the reception." The guests all began to leave their chairs and stream towards an open door where uniformed waiters held trays of champagne.

"What do we do?" asked Meg.

"We came this far. We have to talk to her. We have to find out what she did with that dress."

"You don't think we should come back tomorrow?" It seemed a little presumptuous to grill the bride on her wedding day about a dress she had not even worn.

He shook his head. "Tomorrow she'll be on her honeymoon. If she decided not to wear that dress for whatever reason she's probably happy to sell it."

So, they followed the rest of the guests. Which was a little awkward since they didn't know anyone. But Dylan, as she had noticed, had amazing social skills. Soon they were chatting with another young couple who seemed perfectly happy to accept them. She imagined that people on the bride's side suspected they were with the groom and people who knew the groom imagined they were the bride's friends. Fortunately, it wasn't very long before the bride and groom entered the room.

Meg could see why Tasmine had chosen the gown that she had.

Unlike the fairytale creation that Evangeline had designed, this dress was much simpler and suited her in a way the designer dress would not. It was a graceful A-line gown with a simple scooped neck. On her statuesque body it looked stunning. Her hair was piled high on her head with tiny rosebuds tucked here and there.

She wore a string of pearls around her neck and, like her bridesmaid, carried a simple bouquet of flowers. But the most amazing feature of her whole outfit was her smile. She had a smile like a movie star's and she couldn't seem to stop it from breaking out. This woman exuded happiness. Just looking at her made Meg want to smile too.

She and her new husband walked around mingling with their guests. Accepting congratulations and hugs and kisses. The day was so beautiful that the doors were thrown open and many of the guests drifted outdoors. Delaying the inevitable moment when she and Dylan would be discovered to be fraudulent guests she tugged on his arm and they walked outside. The bridesmaid was already there and standing with her was a man who looked vaguely familiar. She sucked in a breath as she realized who it was. "Oh, my gosh, that's Bennett Saegar, the screenwriter."

"I'd be really impressed if I knew a single screenwriter in Hollywood." Dylan said.

"He's amazingly talented. And he keeps appearing on the list of the hottest bachelors in LA."

"I don't think so, not anymore," Dylan said, and then she noticed the shiny gold band on Bennett's wedding ring finger.

"Wow. He's married. To the bridesmaid?"

"I think she's called matron of honor if she's already married."

"Look at you with your wedding etiquette."

She headed towards the couple and Dylan said, "You think he needs an agent?"

"No. I want to tell them how much I love his work." Then she grinned at him. "And naturally I will mention that I work for a top film and literary agency in case he should happen to need representation."

She walked up to the couple who seemed almost equally in love as the two that had married today. She said, "Bennett Saegar?"

He turned and gave her the kind of smile that a celebrity gives when he's about to be asked for an autograph. He nodded.

She said, "I'm Megan O'Reilly, we met at the premiere of your last movie. I'm an agent with RGW. I think you're tremendously talented."

She saw him ease up immediately. Probably because she was someone in the business and not a woman approaching him because of his status as a hot bachelor in LA.

He put an arm around the woman beside him. "I don't think you've met my wife? This is Ashley."

They shook hands and then she introduced Dylan.

"You must be one of Eric's friends," Ashley said, looking at them both with a slightly puzzled expression.

"Eric?"

Her puzzlement turned to suspicion. "Eric Van Hoffendam? The groom?"

"No. I've never met him."

There was no point in lying to these people and, now that she'd given her name, she felt the only possible course of action was the truth. She said, "We came to see Tasmine. We had no idea there was a wedding going on today and then suddenly found ourselves seated watching the ceremony."

"Really?"

Ashley didn't call for security, but Meg had the feeling she'd better explain fast. She said, "I know this will sound crazy but she brought a dress into the vintage store where Dylan works. The most beautiful wedding gown you've ever seen. It was designed by Evangeline, you know? The famous wedding gown designer?"

Ashley's eyes twinkled and she no longer looked as though she were about to call security. "Oh, I know that gown."

"You do? Do you know what Tasmine did with it?"

"She did exactly what you said she did. She took it to a vintage store in LA."

Meg shook her head. "She did, but then yesterday she took it away again."

Ashley looked confused. "I don't think so. You saw the dress she was wearing. It wasn't an Evangeline gown. Her dress is by an up-and-coming local designer that I introduced her to..

"Meg was feeling increasingly baffled when the bride herself, still holding hands with the groom, arrived to stand with their little group.

"Hi," Tasmine said looking at Meg and Dylan. "You must be Eric's friends?" She glanced at her husband and he looked plain confused.

It was Ashley who answered, briefly retelling a shortened version of the story that Meg had told her.

Tasmine wrinkled her nose. "Why would I want that dress back?"

# CHAPTER 15

*D*ylan took out his smartphone and pulled up one of the photos. He held out the phone.

It was one of her favorite pictures from the photo shoot and showed Megan in that gorgeous gown and him slipping the ring on her finger. Tasmine squinted at the phone in the bright light and nodded. "Yes. I brought the dress into your store. I remember you now. And I think your mother said you'd put it in a window display. Between that and this advertising I can't believe it didn't sell." She glanced at Meg. "You look great in that dress, by the way."

She didn't seem too worried about not getting her money, more surprised.

"There was a lot of interest in the gown," Dylan said. "But, you see, Meg wants to buy it. We held onto it because it was bringing a lot of business into Joe's Past and Present and then yesterday someone came in wanting the dress. My aunt was in charge of the store, it was the last hour of business, and she was helping other customers. She took it down from the display window and put it in a changing room and never saw the dress again. Afterwards, she found a note in the dressing room that said, 'This dress is mine. I'm taking it back.'"

"And you thought that was me?"

"Seemed like a logical conclusion."

Tasmine smiled wryly. "It was never really my dress. I never thought of it as my dress." She turned to her matron of honor. "It was Ashley's dress."

Ashley had worn the wedding dress? It was strange, but Meg wanted to think that no one but her was meant for that dress.

Ashley shook her head. "Don't look at me, I didn't take it. It was a hand-me-down when I got it. In fact, if it's anyone's dress it was the first bride's. Kate's."

Meg felt completely confused. "The first bride? How many are there?"

Ashley sighed. "Well, it all started when Kate Winton- Jones was supposed to marry my cousin, Edward Carnarvon. Evange-line designed that gown for Kate but, frankly, Kate never liked it. It didn't really suit her. Not the way it looks on you. And Ted Carnarvon turned out to have a bit of a secret life. So, she fell in love with an old friend of Ted's and they ran off together before the wedding. You keeping up?"

"I think so."

"Then, Eric here proposed to me. And, since I was always the girl in the family who got the hand-me-downs, my aunt and uncle gave me Kate's dress."

Meg glanced at the two couples. "Okay, maybe I'm not keeping up after all. Eric just married Tasmine. I saw it."

"Correct. But first I was engaged to Eric." She grinned. "And Tasmine was supposed to be my bridesmaid."

Dylan said, "This is starting to sound like *Who's on First*."

"I know. So," here Ashley looked a little bashful and glanced at her new husband, "when I fell in love with Ben, well, I wasn't as sure of myself as Kate was and I sort of left it until the last minute to make up my mind."

Eric said, "Oh, yeah."

Tasmine turned to Meg. "The guests were assembled, the string quartet was playing, Eric was waiting at the altar, we bridesmaids were all ready to go and there was no bride. I ran back to check on Ashley and caught her climbing out the window."

"It's true." Ashley glanced at both of them. "Sorry, Eric."

Eric shook his very handsome head. "No. It's me who's sorry. But that's a long story."

Tasmine continued, "Anyway, there was the bride climbing out the window with Ben waiting for her in a sports car and I helped her out of her dress and she handed me the gown and said, 'Here, this is yours.'"

"The poor dress," Meg said, wishing she'd been there.

"I know. No one else wanted it. Ashley's mother wanted the dress out of the house and her aunt wanted it off the property and so I ended up with it."

"But why didn't you get married in it? It's a stunning gown."

"I know. It is. But Ashley was supposed to wear it. It would have felt so strange to marry Eric in a gown that was supposed to be worn by his previous fiancée."

Meg felt extremely puzzled. "So, how many brides has this dress been through? And has anyone ever worn it down the aisle?"

Ashley and Tasmine exchanged a glance. "I guess you don't know about the curse."

This was starting to sound like horror movie. "The curse?"

They both nodded solemnly. And neither Eric nor Bennett seemed to find the story strange or unusual. She looked at Dylan to reassure herself that someone apart from her thought this was the craziest story they'd ever heard and was pretty sure he was having the same reaction she was.

Ashley picked up the tale. "When Kate was being fitted for that dress, the designer, Evangeline, who is a complete diva and impossible to deal with, shouted at some underling. The woman had accidentally jabbed Kate with a pin because she was so nervous with Evangeline standing over her like the wrath of God, and a tiny spot of blood leaked through the fabric.

"Well, according to Kate, Evangeline completely lost it and screamed at the poor seamstress who then rose up like some creature of mythology and cursed the dress and then cursed Evangeline. Then she stormed out."

"After she cursed the dress?"

"Yes. Of course, everybody pretended it never happened, and who believes in curses anyway, but it was kind of strange that Kate didn't end up getting married in that dress. And then I didn't end up getting married in it."

Tasmine nodded. "And then I didn't end up wearing it."

"So, you're saying that anyone who gets the dress doesn't end up getting married?"

"Not to the person they're engaged to. Not so far."

Tasmine took Eric's hand. "It's kind of spooky, isn't it?"

"But *I* want to get married in that dress!" she exclaimed. "Show them the pictures again Dylan. That dress was made for me!"

Once more he passed the phone. Ashley flipped through the photos on Dylan's phone and nodded. She passed the phone to Tasmine who gazed at the pictures and said, "I have to agree. It looks fabulous on you."

"It looked like crap on me," Ashley said. "And Kate never liked it. Maybe this is your dress. Maybe that's why none of us ever wore it, because it was meant for you."

When Bennett stared at her, she shrugged. "What? It's okay to believe in curses but not that something's meant to be?"

Dylan said, "Whether it's meant to be or not, there's one problem. The dress has disappeared."

Bennett spoke up. "In the note, the person who took it said it was their dress. Do you think Kate took it back? I suppose it was really her dress."

Ashley shook her head. "Kate's happily married to someone else. Why would she want a wedding gown?"

Then Ashley stared at Meg, her eyes and mouth both opening at once. "Maybe it was Evangeline."

"Evangeline? The dress designer?"

Ashley nodded. "Kate says she's an absolute nightmare, and a total control freak. Do you know she won't even design a dress unless she thinks the bride is beautiful enough? What do you bet she saw her gown being advertised on a website and found out it was sitting in a second-hand clothing store. I bet she freaked."

Tasmine said, "Oh, my gosh, you must be right." She turned to Meg and Dylan looking sympathetic. "Maybe if she and the dress are both cursed, it's better this way."

"You think she wants that gown out of circulation?" Dylan asked.

"I don't know. But honestly, do a Google search of her name. There are nasty rumors spreading about that woman and it's pretty clear that her business is suffering. The more times the dress gets passed on, and rumors of the curse go viral, the more her business suffers. How many brides are going to flock to pay way too much money to a wedding gown designer who might be cursed."

"People believe in that stuff?"

"I would have said I didn't believe in curses, but it's true, not one of us has got married in that gown."

"Wow." Meg felt deflated somehow. She said to Dylan, "I don't know what to do now."

Tasmine said, sounding like she was about to cheer on a winning team, "I know what you should do now. You're going to come and join the party. There's tons of food and champagne and there's going to be dancing. Maybe none of us got married in that dress but it did bring us all together. And that's a good thing."

She glanced at Dylan and he shrugged. "Why not?"

It wasn't like they could track down the dress designer today, and even if they did, what would they say to her? No doubt, if she was behind the wedding dress theft she had the gown tucked away in a dungeon somewhere waiting for the rumors of the curse to die down.

"Thank you. We didn't mean to crash your wedding."

"It was Evangeline who brought you here. Even though I never got married in that dress, I'm going to miss it."

As the only one who hadn't had the chance not to get married in the famous gown, Meg felt a bit sorry for herself. But, she supposed, if she had to choose between Dylan and the dress, Dylan was going to win every time. She had just really hoped to have both.

There was no head table at this wedding and no pre-assigned seating so the six of them sat together. Tasmine said to Ben and Ashley, "Are you going to get up and talk?"

"Maybe."

Tasmine leaned toward Meg. "We decided that instead of a lot of formal, boring speeches, we're having an open mic."

Dylan chuckled. "Like a roast?"

Eric nodded. "Probably turn into one." Then he shook his head. "I don't think my parents are having a very good time."

"They like a more formal occasion." Tasmine kissed him. "But this is our day."

Eric squeezed her shoulder and rose. "I'd better start things off," he said, and walked in his slow, easy way to the mic. He stood for a moment until the noise died down. "Tasmine and I want to thank you all for coming today. As most of you know, not so long ago I was all set to marry Ashley Carnarvon."

Meg choked on her champagne. Was he really going to talk about his last girlfriend in front of his brand new wife? She glanced at Tasmine and Ashley but they both looked as though they were waiting for the punch line to a joke. Eric continued, "Some of you were even at the wedding. When Ben Saegar stole her from under my nose." He pointed a finger at Bennett and said, "Dude!"

Bennett shrugged, but looked pretty pleased with himself.

There were titters of embarrassed laughter and then Eric said, "Well, as you can all see, Ashley and I are still what we were always meant to be, which is lifelong friends. And she's found the man of her dreams. Sure, he's a guy who makes stuff up for living, but he makes her happy. And if Ashley and I hadn't been engaged, and Tasmine hadn't been one of her bridesmaids, then I never would have met the woman who turned my life around."

He cleared his throat and Meg felt him come into his own as he said, "I did some stupid things. And Tasmine saw, through the screw-up I was, to the man she believed I could become. To have someone who genuinely believes you can be better is the most powerful thing in the world. Tasmine, you make me want to be the man you deserve and I want you to be the woman by my side for the rest of my life. Thank you for loving me."

Tasmine beamed at him through teary eyes.

Judge Bailey got up next. He was a very formal man, old and fierce looking. As his gaze swept the room Meg found herself straightening her napkin on her lap and making sure she was sitting up properly. He said, "Mrs. Bailey and I have watched this young couple grow together and help each other mostly right here in our home. I didn't think much of Eric at first, but when a man saves your life, you look at him differently."

He raised his glass to Eric. "So it seemed fitting that they get married right here. I don't know how many of you know that Eric has begun his own landscaping company and when you look around at the new garden where the wedding was held you can see his most recent project."

The older man grinned. "I'm not here to do a sales pitch, but if anyone wants to hire a creative and very hard-working young man, I'd be happy to give a reference. And Tasmine represents a line of excellent furniture. If you're interested, you'll find two rooms she decorated and furnished upstairs in the house. My wife and I only met these two a few months back, but we've grown to love them both." He took a moment and she had the odd feeling that he was choked up, probably for one of the few times in his life, he said, "God bless you both."

Meg stared at Eric, who was looking bashful. "You saved his life?"

He shrugged. "He pretty much saved mine, too."

A Hispanic man got up next and said, "My name is Jose. I've been the head gardener here for many years. I didn't like that young punk when he first showed up. And then he started coming up with these highfalutin ideas for the landscaping. I didn't like him or his ideas. But, he worked hard and some of his ideas are okay. Eric, mi amigo, you're all right." Then he shook his head, "But how you got that hot bride I will never know."

Amidst the laughter and clapping Jose sat down and gave his very pretty wife a smacking kiss.

As the speeches and toasts and roasts continued, Meg felt warmth grow within her. Even though these people were strangers to her she could almost see the whole story of Tasmine and Eric's love affair. The disasters and the bumps and the hope and determination that had brought them together.

Even though her heart was broken about the missing dress, she couldn't help but enjoy the wedding of two people so clearly in love with each other. And she felt a kind of sisterhood with these other women who had almost worn that wedding gown she still thought of as hers.

When she and Dylan left later that afternoon, she had contact information for both Ashley and Tasmine, who was headed off on a honeymoon the next day, but wanted to hear how everything had gone when she returned in two weeks time.

As they drove away, Dylan said, "I'm sorry we didn't find the dress, but that was surprisingly fun."

"I know. I can imagine staying friends with those couples. They seem like our kind of people." Even as she said our kind of people she realized that she and Dylan had begun acting like a couple.

"Do you think I'll ever see that dress again?"

He hesitated, then said, "Does it matter so much?"

How could she explain this feeling she had. Finally, she said, "It might have been bad luck for those other women, but for some reason, I think it only brings me good luck."

"Then let's get your lucky charm back."

# CHAPTER 16

$\mathcal{A}$s they drove back, Dylan said, "Okay with you if we stop by Joe's? Mom and Janet will be waiting to hear what happened."

"Sure. Of course. Maybe Joe even has some ideas about how we might handle Evangeline."

The store was closed when they drew up but Dylan let himself in with a key. The two owners were rearranging inventory. They had a series of vintage garments, all French and from the twenties, that Janet had brought back with her. Clearly these were destined to be the new window display. From somewhere, they'd even unearthed bobbed wigs so that the mannequins would have authentic hairstyles.

Joe dropped what she was doing and came rushing forward when they walked into the store. She glanced from one to the other. "Well? Did you find her? You were gone so long, I hope you got the dress?"

Janet ran up to join them, a black satin gown draped over her arm and a fan of pins sticking out of her mouth. She made a mumbling sound, which Meg assumed was her way of asking how it had gone.

She and Dylan looked at each other. Dylan spoke, "We did find Tasmine Ford. But she doesn't have the dress."

Joe wrinkled her nose. "Are you sure? She could still be selling it online. I looked myself but no Evangeline gown seems to be listed for sale on any of the big sites."

He shook his head. "No. In fact, we crashed Tasmine's wedding."

A spray of pins shot from Janet's mouth like tiny missiles as she burst into laughter. "You crashed a wedding? I haven't done that in years. Is it still as much fun?"

She turned to Meg. "There's something so delicious about a wedding, isn't there? Especially if you don't actually know the people."

She felt that Janet would never cease to amaze her. She said, "Yes, it was fascinating."

"I bet Tasmine didn't look half as good as you in that dress," Janet said.

"I don't know. She wasn't wearing it."

"What? She steals a wedding gown and then doesn't wear it? What is the girl, crazy?"

Dylan shook his head. "She didn't take it back. She thinks the person we're looking for is the designer herself."

Joe took a step back. "Evangeline? You think Evangeline stole back her own dress?"

Dylan turned to Janet. "That woman who tried on the dress last, do you remember what she looked like? Or whether she had an accent?"

Janet narrowed her eyes as she thought back to the day the gown went missing. "I think she had dark hair. And maybe an Australian accent?"

"Could it have been British?"

"Sure. We didn't talk much."

She, Dylan, and Joe all nodded. "Evangeline is British."

"But, why didn't she say who she was and what she wanted? All she had to do was ask."

"It was probably a completely mortifying experience for her," Joe said. She of course would have recognized Evangeline right away from her years in the fashion and modeling world. "We worked together a few times in London and New York. She was already a diva back then. Of course, she was much more successful than I was, although if you ask me, she was more interested in using beauty and fame to snag rich men than to model clothes and makeup."

She shook her head. "She was so beautiful: eyes that were the color of good sapphires, flawless skin, and a kind of attitude she emanated that drew them all to her. But she had a terrible reputation in the business. Demanding, difficult, always shouting at somebody."

"Did she ever marry any of those rich men?" Meg wondered aloud.

"She was engaged once, I think. She lived with a movie star, and then I believe a rich Russian oligarch bought her a townhouse in London. But, as far as I know, she never married any of them."

"It's almost sad."

"I think, for her to come and ask for one of her gowns back from a secondhand store? It would be so beneath her she couldn't even contemplate it. Especially if she knew the store was mine."

"So she stole the gown instead? That's not beneath her?"

"I'm not justifying her actions. I'm just trying to understand what happened." She touched Meg's shoulder. "If Evangeline does have the gown, I doubt you'll ever get it now, Meg. I'm so sorry."

She wasn't nearly ready to give up. She was going to find a way to get to this Evangeline. There had to be something they could do.

When they went to leave Dylan said, "What's this?" He bent down and picked up an envelope that had been pushed under the door. "This wasn't here when we came in."

He handed it to Joe. There was no writing on the front. She opened the flap and looked inside. Her eyebrows rose. Without saying a word she withdrew a slim sheaf of notes. She fanned them out. Five crisp, new, one-thousand-dollar bills.

# CHAPTER 17

"Well, I guess we can take theft off the list," Dylan said, looking at the five grand. "There's no note?"

"Nothing but the money."

"That's good," Janet said. "We'll still get our commission, and the brand-new bride will have a nice chunk of change to start her new married life. All's well that ends well."

It hadn't ended very well for Meg. She still had no wedding dress.

She could not escape the feeling that somehow she had become caught up in a spell. From the moment she'd seen that dress hanging in the window of Joe's Past and Present, Meg had been bewitched, dazzled by a vision of herself that had become so strong she had believed she could make it true.

She had spent so much of her life in fictional worlds that an unpleasant suspicion grew in her mind that she had created one of her own. Now that the dress had disappeared, she wondered if, like Cinderella after the clock struck midnight, she'd go back to her very humdrum life. Dylan would see her, not as the dress had made her, but as she really was.

When he caught a glimpse of her face, he said, "Come on, it's only a dress."

But, as the magic faded, her sense of herself as a woman who deserved a designer wedding gown and who deserved to walk down the aisle to marry someone as amazing as Dylan began to recede too.

She said, "Do you think we're rushing things?"

He turned to her and she saw an expression of hurt cross his eyes. "No. I don't feel like we're rushing. I feel like everything is starting to make sense."

"What if we're wrong? What if what we're doing makes no sense at all? Maybe the dress going missing is a sign that we should take things easy. Back it up a step."

"Okay, when you say back it up a step, what does that mean exactly?"

She had no idea what she meant. Only that she did not want Dylan to end up feeling trapped because she wasn't the person he believed her to be. Of course, it was impossible to explain this. "I don't know what I mean. Maybe we should just slow down a bit." She didn't want to believe in curses, but it was strange that each of the brides who touched the Evangeline gown didn't end up marrying the guy they were engaged to.

"Could we forget that I semi-proposed to you in the car today?" he asked.

Yeah, it was already beginning. The magic was receding and he was beginning to see that she was a very ordinary woman, not one you wanted to tumble into love and marriage with. She nodded. "Consider the incident erased from my mind."

Of course, that magical and slightly humorous proposal would never be erased from her mind. She felt that she would polish up the memory and put it on a special shelf where she could bring it out in years ahead to remind her of one of the most amazing periods of her life.

He said, "What if we go get some gelato and watch a movie or something."

She shook her head slowly. "I think I need to go home to my own place. I've got to buckle down and go through more manuscripts and, well, I need some time alone."

"Fine. I understand."

"If I hadn't come into the store that day and tried on the wedding dress, I mean, suppose we had met at a party somewhere, do you think you would have noticed me?"

He appeared to give the matter some thought. He said, "I don't know." He smiled a little and she was positive he was reliving that moment when she first tried on the wedding dress and he'd helped her do up the buttons. When their gazes had first connected in the triple mirror and she had felt almost as though lightning had struck her. Maybe the force of the current had gone through her body, through his fingers touching her skin and into his, infecting him with the same magic or witchery. "But," he continued, "I'm really glad it happened the way it did." Then he looked slightly thunderstruck. "Do you think we've already been at the same events and didn't notice each other?"

That was a depressing thought. "In a city like LA? It's possible."

He shook his head. "Fate has a funny way of getting involved in our lives, doesn't it?"

"It does." And she wondered if he considered fate a positive force or a negative force. She hated herself for being this insecure, and refused to ask the question. But if that dress was cursed, and doomed to split up couples, what hope was there for her and Dylan?

When she got home, she couldn't shake the feeling that as crazy as it was, she'd had some kind of a spell cast on her and now it was fading. June was obviously home since music played softly from her bedroom. A pang of guilt struck her; she hadn't even opened June's book file. She'd printed off a hard copy at the office and not done another thing.

She crept into her bedroom and then realized she was acting like a coward. She emerged and yelled, "Hey!" They always greeted each other when they arrived home and said goodbye when they left. She didn't want to be rude just because she hadn't had time to read June's manuscript.

"Hey, yourself," June answered. She came out of her room. She was wearing sweats and it wasn't a post-workout kind of look. Meg had the feeling that she had been writing.

She was about to apologize and promise that she was going to open the book file right away when June looked at her in some concern. "What happened? You look like somebody ran over your puppy."

"Well, no animals were harmed. But, I have suffered a terrible loss."

June had her moments, and this was one of them, when she proved herself to be fantastic roommate. "Ice cream or tea?"

"No, really. You're busy and I don't really want to talk about it."

June shook her head so her ponytail bounced. "That's not how it works. You know what they say, a trouble shared is a trouble halved. Cut in two. Something like that."

"Who says that? I think the opposite is true. The more you talk about something the worse it seems."

"Well, I'm sick of looking at my computer screen and you look like you need a friend. We can talk about anything."

June pointed to the kettle sitting on the counter with one hand and to the freezer with the other and raised her eyebrows. Meg said, "Tea."

"Good. Tea suggests the trouble is fixable. And not the true heartbreak of a rocky road moment."

"We have rocky road?"

But June thought she was joking and put the kettle on.

She took the time to go to her room, dump her stuff and throw on her own sweats, then she returned to their main living area and flopped on the couch.

June brought over her tea in a mug that proclaimed World's Greatest Actress. June was big on positive thinking. There was no mug in the cupboard for World's Number One Agent. She wondered if such a mug existed. Maybe most agents didn't need the ego boost.

June settled on the opposite side of the couch. "Well? What do you want to talk about?"

It was pretty obvious she didn't want to talk about local politics or the environment so she said, "This is going to sound crazy. But, you know the Evangeline wedding gown?"

"Sure I do. You fell in love with it, and you fell in love with the guy in the vintage store, and then when I went to try the dress on, he didn't even want to let me touch it."

"Well, the gown has been stolen."

June sat up so fast she slopped tea on her gray Berkeley sweatshirt. She never understood quite why June had that sweatshirt since she had not attended Berkeley. Given how big it was, she thought it might have belonged to a previous boyfriend.

"Who would steal a wedding dress? Can you imagine the bad karma? I bet whoever stole that dress is cursed."

As miserable as she was, Meg had to laugh. "You are exactly right. It seems very likely that the person who stole the dress is Evangeline herself."

June's eyes opened wide. "No way."

"I don't know this for sure. And don't even think about blogging about this. But we think it was her."

"Why would a famous dress designer steal back her own stuff out of a vintage store?"

"Dylan and I thought that girl who brought the dress in for

consignment was the one who took it back. When we tracked her down, well, we sort of crashed her wedding."

June snorted with laughter. "You, the most well-mannered person I know, crashed a wedding? I think I'll more easily believe that a dress was cursed than that you would crash a wedding."

"Well, they are sort of related." And then she told the story of how she and Dylan had inadvertently attended the wedding of Tasmine Ford and Eric Van Hoffendam. June asked the odd question but mostly she listened as the tale unfolded.

When she was done, June said, "So, let me get this straight. This chick gets a super expensive wedding gown designed by Evangeline. During a fitting the dress and Evangeline get cursed, and this chick doesn't get married in it."

"Right. And then the dress gets passed on to the groom's cousin, and she doesn't get married in the dress either."

"And then, in a super strange twist of events, the bridesmaid from wedding two gets given the gown, ends up marrying the groom jilted by the cousin, is this right?"

"Yes. And then, because she wasn't going to wear it, because of her groom being the jilted groom thing, she brought the dress into Dylan's store. And that's where I fell in love with both Dylan and the dress."

June settled back and sipped more tea. "I don't think you should be sad that this wedding dress is gone out of your life. Think about it. Every bride who was supposed to wear that dress didn't end up marrying the guy. Meg, that thing is cursed."

This was not what she wanted to hear. "So, you think I'll never marry Dylan?"

"What? You've known him like a month! What's all this about marriage?"

She really did need a friend to talk this through with. She took a sip of her tea and liked the soothing warmth in her throat. "It's been like a dream, or a fantasy. When I wore that dress in front of him something amazing happened. And now the dress is gone and I feel like the magic is gone."

June was shaking her head violently. "No. A hundred times no! You get that dress far away from you and don't ever touch it again. Think about it. Girls who wear that dress don't get married to the guy they start out with, which means you would never marry Dylan in that dress. That is some serious, scary curse."

All Meg had ever felt was happiness when she'd stepped into that gown. "But, if something's cursed, wouldn't you get a feeling about it? The feeling I got when I wore that dress was that everything was magical. I didn't feel like a single woman in LA with a crappy job. I didn't feel like a girl who had bad luck with romance. I felt beautiful and desirable and confident."

"You sure that was the dress?"

She glanced over at June. "What else could it be?"

"If Dylan looked at me the way he looks at you? I think I'd feel pretty sexy and beautiful and confident too. I think you're looking in the wrong place for your magic."

"Wow. I never thought of it that way . . ."

"You're welcome."

Meg finished her tea and said, "You're a good friend."

"I try to be."

And because June was a good friend she said, "I am really sorry I haven't had a chance to start your manuscript yet. But I'm going to do it right now. But, before I start I need to tell you something."

"Okay. What?"

She took a deep breath, realizing that June wasn't her old boyfriend and she wasn't going to pretend to like something she didn't. "I'm not going to blow smoke. I'm going to be really honest, as though your book were any submission to the agency."

"Absolutely. That's what I want."

"Then you have to promise me that if I don't love the book we will still be friends."

June gaped at her. "Do you think I've spent five years in this town going to auditions for everything from dog food commercials to tampon ads to feature films without learning how to handle rejection? Give me your worst. All you can do is make me a better writer."

She felt a huge weight lift off her chest. "Okay. Deal."

# CHAPTER 18

*D*ylan stepped into Joe's Past and Present like a man
with a mission.

Both his mother and his aunt were in the store. He walked
up to his mother and, obviously seeing his agitation, Janet came
forward to hear what was going on. He supposed that was one
of the qualities that made her books so popular. She never
minded pushing her nose in on other people's business. But, he
loved her and he knew she had his best interests at heart so he
welcomed her into their little circle. He said, "Mom, you still
have a lot of contacts in the fashion industry. I need to get hold
of Evangeline. We need to get that dress back."

Joe was already shaking her head. "I told you, I've worked
with her a few times. Frankly, I doubt she would even
remember me, and she was always difficult. I doubt she's
become any easier to deal with, especially, if what those women
at the wedding told you is true."

"Oh, it's true all right." He went to the computer that they
kept behind the cash desk and pulled up a notorious gossip
blog. He read a few choice quotes from the articles he'd already

scanned. Headlines like, "Pretty Satin Can't Hide the Fact that Evangeline is Cursed!"

"Wow, I never liked the woman, but that's cruel."

"I know. It's mostly this one guy. Dixon. He's got a blog and he strings for the worst of the gossip rags. Somebody's feeding him information because he's getting the inside scoop on clients canceling their orders for wedding gowns and how much her business is suffering."

Joe leaned over his shoulder and perused the screen. "Do you think it's true?"

Dylan shrugged. "Doesn't matter if it's true or not, if enough brides believe it, her business will be doomed."

Janet asked, "Honey, why is it so important to get that dress back? Sounds to me it should be purified with holy water and buried."

He shook his head. He didn't understand it himself, but he knew that for Meg the Evangeline wedding gown was so much more than simply a dress. She had imbued it with qualities of magic and promise. Like someone who loses their lucky medallion or their four-leafed clover, he felt that if she believed her luck was ending that she'd make it true. And since he knew that she associated them falling in love with that dress, he worried that without the dress she may look differently at him. He tried to explain this to his aunt and his mother but it all sounded lame when he said it aloud.

Janet obviously picked up enough of what he was trying to say. She said, "Maybe I should call Evangeline."

"Why would she talk to you?" Joe asked. Her forehead crinkled as she looked at her sister and Dylan suspected there might be more going on with his aunt than a simple desire to help out her nephew. She said breezily, "I might be in the market for a wedding gown myself."

Dylan and his mother exchanged glances. Like they didn't

have enough problems today. Joe asked, "You're not marrying that French guy, are you?"

"He hasn't asked me but he's flying out here to spend a week with me. If I can still stand him at the end of the week I might marry him."

His mother muttered something under her breath. It might have been a prayer.

"So, if you go and see Evangeline about designing a wedding dress for you, how are you going to persuade her to give us back the stolen one?"

She shook her head. "No. I've given the matter a lot of thought. And, after hearing about the curse, I know I'm right. You and Meg are starting a life together. You don't want that dress. You don't want a wedding gown that three other brides have almost worn. What you want is a brand new dress. I think Evangeline should design one for Meg."

"Of course! That's a great idea. She definitely owes us one." Then he paused to consider. "But, if we were selling a second-hand gown for five grand, I can't even imagine how much an original costs."

"Oh, I can," Janet said. "I've never had children. You're all I've got. I will buy Meg her own Evangeline gown. It's my engagement present to both of you."

His mother interrupted, staring hard at Dylan. "Wait a minute. Since when are you engaged?"

"It was stupid. We got to talking and suddenly I was talking about the future and us being married and before you know it I was sort of proposing."

His aunt's eyes danced with amusement. "Well, do you want to marry Meg?"

"Of course I do. I think I fell in love with her the first time I saw her. She's amazing, and beautiful and smart and doesn't even see how great she is."

Janet looked at Joe. "Sounds like love to me."

"But now the dress is gone, I think she's having second thoughts."

Janet made a sound like *Bah*, which he suspected she got from her new French boyfriend. She said, "That girl is so crazy about you it's beautiful to watch. But what you need, my darling nephew, is to do the job properly. It wasn't the wedding dress going missing that messed things up. It was your bumbling accidental proposal. When a woman receives a proposal—" and she glanced at both of them in a rather coquettish manner, "and believe me, I know, I've been proposed to many a time—she wants to feel that she's the most important person in the world." She sighed a little. "Even with the men who proposed to me whom I had no intention of marrying, I still enjoyed the magic of the moment. Now, a woman likes her man to do certain things when he proposes to her."

Dylan had a feeling he'd missed a few critical things when he accidentally proposed. "Should I make a list?"

"That won't be necessary. I think your genius brain can manage to remember two things. First of all, you need an engagement ring. I think you should always make sure it's returnable in case she prefers to choose her own, but there's something about the sparkling diamond presented by a man on bended knee that brings flutters to a woman's heart."

He didn't really like where this was going. "On bended knee? Are you kidding me?"

"It's your way of telling her that your heart is at her feet."

"I don't mind getting a ring."

"Not just any ring. It has to be something that you believe she would love."

Amazingly, he started feeling enthusiastic about this program. There were no jewelry stores open at this time of night, but he felt that he wanted to fix his bungling of things earlier as soon as he could. Suddenly, he had an idea. "Mom!

Those rings that we used in the advertising shoot. You still have them?"

Even Joe was getting into the spirit of the thing. "Yes, that's brilliant. Those rings looked beautiful on her."

"I might have to take the rings on the installment plan, all my savings are invested in our startup costs, but I'll pay you back."

"You take the rings now. Pay me when you have the money."

Janet looked shocked. "Joe, you're not going to make him pay for those rings."

Dylan said, "Sure I am. This is a woman I plan to marry and have children with. I'm buying her the rings."

Janet put up her hands. "Forgive me. You really are a lot like your mother. You have to do everything yourself."

"No. I do accept your engagement gift. If you can get Evangeline to design Meg her own wedding gown, I think everybody would win."

His mother went to the locked case where she kept the most special pieces of jewelry and removed the vintage engagement ring and the wedding ring that went with it. "Do you want both rings, or should I keep the other one safe for you?"

"I'll just take the engagement ring for now." And he really hoped he'd be getting the other ring soon.

The ring sitting in its own tattered blue velvet jewelry box somehow added to its charm. He felt this ring had stories to tell and a history of long and happy marriages and for a woman who loved stories he felt that this was the perfect ring.

"Okay. Got the ring, check." His face was twisted. "Asking on bended knee. But where?"

"Tradition would have you propose in a restaurant with a dozen red roses on the table and champagne already cooling for the moment she says yes."

"I am not getting down on my knees in a crowded restaurant. I'll look like a moron. Anyway, it doesn't feel right."

"Maybe there's another place that's special to the two of you?"

He thought of Griffith Park, but that seemed kind of a cliché too.

And then it hit him. He glanced around. "Here. It has to be here. This is where we met, this is where it all started."

The two older women exchanged glances. Janet shrugged, "Wouldn't float my boat, but there's a certain Bohemian charm to the idea."

His mother got into the spirit of the location more quickly. She said, "What do you need me to do?"

# CHAPTER 19

*M*eg took a deep breath and opened June's book. *Please let it not be very bad. Please let me find something positive to say.* It was titled, *A Cherry Blossom Floats to LA.*

Interesting title. Curious, she began reading. "There's a saying in China that when you trim the oil lamp the picture becomes clear. What the Chinese mean by this, I think, is that when you share a story with a friend you begin to understand that story better. This is my story, but before that it's the story of my mother and her mother and hers."

Somehow, Meg had expected the book to be a pastiche, as though June might have slapped together her blog posts into some kind of order. But what she'd done was to create a fictional memoir of woman who was from Chinese roots and yet had never seen China. She was half American and yet never felt completely American, either. She wove the history of two families with her experiences being a contemporary single woman and dating in LA.

June's trademark snarky humor broke through and Meg found herself chuckling in more than one place. But, like all good comic novelists, she also touched on dark themes of sacrifice, death and tragedy. It wasn't a perfect book, but the tips of Meg's fingers began to tingle with excitement. She read on, unable to believe that the book she'd dreaded reading was one of the freshest and most compelling reads she'd come across in more than a year. Her heart pounded, almost as though she were falling in love. It was like destiny tapping her on the shoulder and saying, "Here I am."

Even as she read, her agent's mind was checking off boxes. The novel was a humorous portrayal of a contemporary mixed-race woman in a society where she felt she didn't quite fit. It contained the broader story of a young single woman struggling to find her identity, her place in the world, and hopefully true love. Great marketing hooks.

After a while there was a knock on her door. "I'm getting sushi, you want some?" June asked.

She was starving she realized. "Yes, please." She was about to tell June how excited she was but decided to wait until she'd read a little more.

She couldn't have said whether June brought her in a plate of California rolls or raw eel. She ate, and she read.

When she finished the book, she felt a sense of a woman still lost, but also filled with hope. She sat for a moment and breathed in and then she walked out of her bedroom and found June in the living room. Something about her posture told Meg that she'd been sitting there as nervously as an expectant father in a maternity waiting room.

She had an open magazine on her knee, her laptop on the table, a newspaper next to her, and Meg knew she wasn't concentrating on any of them.

She said, very calmly, "June? Can you come here for a second?"

June was so surprised that she stood up and walked over to where Meg was standing just behind the kitchen counter. When she drew closer, Meg threw her arms around her friend and screamed, "I love it! I love your novel!"

"Really?"

"I can't even tell you how excited I am about this book. I absolutely want to represent it and you. I think you have a fresh voice and a dynamite story, it's completely marketable, and I am only so, so sorry I didn't read it the second you gave it to me."

Tears were running down June's face as she said, "Oh, my God!"

"I'm shaking I'm so excited."

"Do you think I need to rewrite any of it?" June asked, always the insecure writer.

"There are a couple of rough spots. But we're not changing one single thing. I'm going right in on Monday morning and taking this to my boss. If I'm right, and he loves this as much as I do, this could be a big break for both of us. Your manuscript could be the thing that gets me the promotion."

Then they danced around the kitchen, jumping up and down.

When they'd calmed down a little, she was hit with a burst of inspiration. "I have an idea. Imagine if I went in on Monday, not only with your manuscript, but with a cover quote from the travel writer, Janet Delaney."

"You think she'd like my book?" June seemed stunned that anyone would like her book.

"As I was reading your work, I was reminded of her style—not that you write travel memoir, but that you both catch the essence of what it feels like to be a woman struggling in a culture she doesn't fully understand. To be alone in a world that still doesn't really embrace single women. When we take this out on submission? Having a Janet Delaney cover quote could really help."

"I'm speechless." Then they both screamed a little more and jumped around the kitchen.

When Meg got her breath back, she said, "I'm going to call her right now. Maybe she can read it before Monday morning and give us a quote."

She glanced at the kitchen clock. "Nine isn't too late to call, is it?"

"I don't think so."

Meg dug out her cell phone.

"I was supposed to go to a party, but I was too nervous. I knew you were reading my book and I couldn't leave until I knew what you thought of it. But now? Now it's time to party!"

Meg laughed. "You go party, you've earned it. But," she held up her forefinger, "do not tell a single soul about this manuscript. Everybody in LA is connected to somebody else. I want this book to come as a complete surprise to my boss. Believe me, it won't be long and you'll have lots to shout about."

She nodded. "I think I'm too scared to jinx it. I'll keep everything you said to myself. But hey, thanks."

Before Meg could lose her nerve, she found Janet's phone number, which Dylan's aunt had given her when she'd proposed lunch. She called Janet's cell and after couple rings, the woman picked up. "Hello?"

"Hi, Janet. It's Meg. Meg O'Reilly."

"Dylan's Meg?" Janet sounded stunned to hear from her.

"Yes, and I'm sorry if I'm calling you at a bad time."

"No. It's a good time. What can I do for you, Meg?"

"It's a crazy request, but I just read a manuscript that blew me away. I'd love to send it to you, I think you'll love it. It's by a brand-new writer, she's a young woman with a comedic voice that strangely reminded me of yours. If you like the book, would you consider giving her a cover quote?"

There was a tiny pause. "I rarely do this, but because it's you, and because I feel bad that I couldn't give you my business, I will read the manuscript. But I make no promises. If I don't like it, I'm not giving her a quote."

"Absolutely. I appreciate your professionalism and thank you so much. Can I email you her manuscript? Or, I've got a printed copy if you prefer."

She thought she heard whispering going on. Then, Janet said, "I'd prefer the printed version. Can you bring it over now?"

She punched the air. "Absolutely. What's your address?"

"Bring it to Joe's Past and Present. I'll be there in a half-hour."

Did Janet not want her to know where she lived? Or were she and Joe still working at the store? Whatever, she was so happy that Janet had agreed to read the book. She was positive she'd be blown away.

She had the pleasure of being able to tell June, as she headed out the door, that Janet had agreed to read the manuscript.

"This night just keeps getting better and better."

"Maybe you'll meet the love of your life tonight, and that will inspire you to write the sequel."

"Maybe."

Because Janet was always so elegantly turned out, Meg got out of her comfy sweats and put on her best jeans and a pretty top. Even though she'd only see Janet for a minute, she felt it was important to look her best, so she spent her remaining time brushing out her hair, brushing her teeth, and freshening her makeup. Then she grabbed the manuscript and headed out.

She pulled up in front of the store and took a moment to rehearse what she'd say. As though Janet had been watching for her, she opened the door as soon as Meg reached it. She looked as excited as though she was about to jump out from behind a couch and yell 'Surprise!'

Meg could hear soft music playing from inside the store and she thought she saw the flickering light of a candle. Her heart began to pound. "What's going on?"

"I'll let Dylan tell you. He's waiting for you inside."

*Dylan? He was here?*

"Okay. Now, the manuscript is not perfect. It's going to need a good edit but—"

"Honey, I'll read the manuscript. You go on in." And then, to Meg's surprise, the woman wrapped her arms around her and hugged her tight. "I'm so excited."

It was amazing to find a jaded writer excited about a brand-new writer's manuscript. She said, "I'm excited too."

And then Janet shut the door on her and she found herself inside the store while Janet was outside and walking away. She followed the glow of candlelight and then there he was.

Dylan. He wore the clothes he'd been wearing the first time she ever met him. The same black T-shirt and jeans. And, like that first day she met him, she felt that hum of recognition.

He'd moved the red velvet couch and put a small table beside it. On the table was a huge bouquet of spring flowers. From somewhere he'd found a silver ice bucket and stand and in it was a bottle of champagne.

Music played softly and in the candlelight Joe's looked mysterious and magical.

He walked towards her and took her face in his hands and kissed her gently, but surely.

"What's going on?" she asked, feeling happy and confused and a bit nervous.

He pulled back slowly and said, "When I make a mistake, I like to fix it as soon as possible."

She swallowed. "Did you make a mistake?"

"Oh yeah, a big one. I fumbled that proposal earlier today so badly. I need to do it again, and do it right."

"Oh, Dylan, are you proposing?" she asked for the second time that day.

"Damn, I think I screwed up again. I really hope I never have to do this again."

She felt her eyes mist even as a smile bloomed so she felt like a human rainbow.

"I hope you never have to do it again either."

"Could you sit?" He indicated the red velvet settee where she'd sat in the Evangeline wedding gown, when they had the advertising photo shoot. She'd never forget that evening.

He sat beside her and took her hand. She'd never seen him so serious. In the flickering light of the candles, she thought he was the most beautiful man she'd ever seen. He said, "It started here. It started here in the store. You walked in, and I looked up and in that moment my life changed forever."

"You felt it too?"

He nodded. "I know we haven't known each other for long, but I've fallen deeper in love every time I see you." He got off the couch and dropped to one knee in front of her.

He dug his hand in his pocket and struggled to retrieve the object that was in there, but from his bent position, it was stuck. "Damn," he mumbled under his breath, and stood up to remove a small box from his pocket before resuming his place on one knee in front of her.

He was so adorable, and she loved him so much. She could barely take in that this was real, and the man of her dreams, a man she'd known only a few weeks, was proposing. He flipped open the ring box and she gasped. "It's the ring, from our photo shoot."

"I told Janet how badly I screwed up, and she said I had to do it again and do it right. She said to find a ring that I felt you would truly love. She also said to make sure it was returnable."

She laughed shakily. "She's a practical woman. And I am never returning this ring."

"The minute she said that, I remembered this ring. And how perfect it looked on your hand, as though it belonged there." She held out her hand and he slipped the ring onto her finger where it sparkled as though it were happy to be there.

He glanced up at her. "I know we don't have the dress, but we do have this." He handed her a wedding album and as she opened it she saw all the photos from their advertising shoot. Candid shots of her in the gown, candids of him in his tux, the pair of them on the settee, him slipping the ring on her finger.

"Meg O'Reilly, will you marry me?"

"Yes." Because in a fairytale ending, there was only one answer.

He got up from the ground and wrapped her in his arms. When he'd kissed her breathless, he said, "I'm sorry about that dress."

She shook her head. "Maybe it's done its job. Maybe it was meant to bring us together."

She leaned forward and kissed him. In the flickering light her ring winked with promise. "And now I'm with you, where I belong."

"Forever," he said, and pulled her into his arms.

Thanks for reading *The Wedding Flight!* Are you ready for the final novel in *The Almost Wives Club* series? Read Evangeline's story— *If the Dress Fits.*

## A Note from Nancy

Dear Reader,

Thank you for reading *The Almost Wives Club* series. I am so grateful for all the enthusiasm this series has received.

I hope you'll consider leaving a review and please tell your friends who like contemporary romance or romantic comedies.

Review on Amazon, Goodreads or BookBub.

Join my newsletter for a free prequel to my *Vampire Knitting Club* series, *Tangles and Treasons*, the exciting tale of how the gorgeous Rafe Crosyer was turned into a vampire.

I hope to see you in my private Facebook Group. It's a lot of fun. www.facebook.com/groups/NancyWarrenKnitwits

Until next time,
Happy Reading,

Nancy

# ALSO BY NANCY WARREN

The best way to keep up with new releases, sales, plus enjoy bonus content and prizes is to join Nancy's newsletter at NancyWarrenAuthor.com or join her private Facebook group www.facebook.com/groups/NancyWarrenKnitwits

## The Almost Wives Club

An enchanted wedding dress is a matchmaker in this series of romantic comedies where five runaway brides find out who the best men really are!

The Almost Wives Club: Kate - Book 1

Second Hand Bride - Book 2

Bridesmaid for Hire - Book 3

The Wedding Flight - Book 4

If the Dress Fits - Book 5

The Almost Wives Club Box Set - Books 1-5

## Take a Chance series

Meet the Chance family, a cobbled together family of eleven kids who are all grown up and finding their ways in life and love.

Chance Encounter - Prequel

Kiss a Girl in the Rain - Book 1

Iris in Bloom - Book 2

Blueprint for a Kiss - Book 3

Every Rose - Book 4

Love to Go - Book 5

The Sheriff's Sweet Surrender - Book 6

The Daisy Game - Book 7

Take a Chance Box Set - Prequel and Books 1-3

### The Vampire Knitting Club

Paranormal Cozy Mysteries. When Lucy inherits her grandmother's knitting shop in Oxford, she discovers secrets and solves murders with the help of some special undead amateur sleuths.

Tangles and Treasons - a free prequel for Nancy's newsletter subscribers

The Vampire Knitting Club - Book 1

Stitches and Witches - Book 2

Crochet and Cauldrons - Book 3

Stockings and Spells - Book 4

Purls and Potions - Book 5

Fair Isle and Fortunes - Book 6

Lace and Lies - Book 7

Bobbles and Broomsticks - Book 8

Popcorn and Poltergeists - Book 9

Garters and Gargoyles - Book 10

Diamonds and Daggers - Book 11

Herringbones and Hexes - Book 12

Ribbing and Runes - Book 13

Cat's Paws and Curses - A Holiday Whodunnit

Vampire Knitting Club Boxed Set: Books 1-3

Vampire Knitting Club Boxed Set: Books 4-6

### The Vampire Book Club

A middle aged witch gets sent to Ireland to run an unusual book shop.

Crossing the Lines - Prequel

The Vampire Book Club - Book 1

Chapter and Curse - Book 2

A Spelling Mistake - Book 3

**The Great Witches Baking Show**

The Great Witches Baking Show - Book 1

Baker's Coven - Book 2

A Rolling Scone - Book 3

A Bundt Instrument - Book 4

Blood, Sweat and Tiers - Book 5

Crumbs and Misdemeanors - Book 6

A Cream of Passion - Book 7

Gingerdead House - A Holiday Whodunnit

The Great Witches Baking Show Boxed Set: Books 1-3

**Toni Diamond Mysteries**

Toni is a successful saleswoman for Lady Bianca Cosmetics in this series of humorous cozy mysteries.

Frosted Shadow - Book 1

Ultimate Concealer - Book 2

Midnight Shimmer - Book 3

A Diamond Choker For Christmas - A Holiday Whodunnit

For a complete list of books, check out Nancy's website at NancyWarrenAuthor.com

# ABOUT THE AUTHOR

Nancy Warren is the USA Today Bestselling author of more than 90 novels. She's originally from Vancouver, Canada, though she tends to wander and has lived in England, Italy and California at various times. While living in Oxford she dreamed up The Vampire Knitting Club. Favorite moments include being the answer to a crossword puzzle clue in Canada's National Post newspaper, being featured on the front page of the New York Times when her book Speed Dating launched Harlequin's NASCAR series, and being nominated three times for Romance Writers of America's RITA award. She has an MA in Creative Writing from Bath Spa University. She's an avid hiker, loves chocolate and most of all, loves to hear from readers! The best way to stay in touch is to sign up for Nancy's newsletter at NancyWarrenAuthor.com or www.facebook.com/groups/NancyWarrenKnitwits

*To learn more about Nancy and her books*
NancyWarrenAuthor.com